"These are tales to make you wonder about the people you know. I thought I knew the author pretty well, but this is worrying."

- Sarah Lattimer

"Comedies dark enough to make readers sleep with a light on."

- Morris Quint

"What *have* you been up to since you left home?"

- The author's mother

Undivulged Crimes

Copyright © Michael Reidy 2019

All rights reserved.

ISBN-13: 978-1974064144

ISBN-10: 197406414X

*Undivulged Crimes
and other Tales*

Lattimer & Co.
PHILADELPHIA • LONDON • PARIS
2019

Undivulged Crimes

For Fiona
actress, poet, teacher, editor

Tremble, thou wretch,
That hast within thee undivulged crimes,
Unwhipp'd of justice
- King Lear, III, ii

Undivulged Crimes

Foreword

These stories were written throughout my working life, from 1971 to the present. Subject, style, and vocabulary have changed over time, as have the things I consider important.

These are not arranged in chronological order, but I will say that "The Magic Shop" is the earliest, and "Angela's Wedding," the latest.

"The" was written in 1985 as a farce. Events have blunted the humour, but I do not believe that we should pretend that the world was any different than it was.

I should make clear that no one in the stories is real, nor is any character based on a single person.

If there is a common thread in these tales, it is that one never knows the history of another person which is why there is a limitless source of stories, and myriad undivulged crimes.

Saint Avit-Frandat

Undivulged Crimes

Extracts of the following works are quoted:
In "The Journal of Nick Carraway," F. Scott Fitzgerald, *The Great Gatsby*, 1925.
In "Undivulged Crimes," "To His Coy Mistress" by Andrew Marvell, 1681; "Patterns" by Amy Lowell, 1916

Contents

The Magic Shop	1
The Return of Colonel Thurston	23
Nick Carraway's Journal	41
The Gemini Experiment	87
The Benefactor	103
The Remarkable Adventure of the Royal Society	135
The Pit	161
Winter Wind	191
Angela's Wedding	223
Undivulged Crimes	237

Undivulged Crimes

The Magic Shop

Undivulged Crimes

The Magic Shop

I discovered the shop on my first day in Barcelona. I suppose that is not curious in itself as it is located close to the cathedral in the Gothic Quarter. This was Barcelona before the area was chic; before the Olympics; before the restoration of the king, when speaking Catalan could have you arrested.

It was the beginning of January. The Spanish were still preparing to celebrate Christmas gift-giving. Row upon row of coloured lights stretched across the Ramblas and tall trees stood in the city squares. In the cloister of the cathedral a crèche was set up and geese waddled around Maria y José under the palm trees.

After wandering through the church, I went down the great steps and into a narrow street where the crowds of people and the brightness of Christmas had not penetrated. The street was lined with extravagant antique shops which seemed to be conducting business as usual, with only the occasional wreath or token group of coloured candles giving indication of the coming holiday.

It was then that I first saw the shop. It stood out because its front was of red lacquered wood shaped into a large art nouveau pattern. I looked into its windows. Neatly, but unimaginatively displayed were a dead rat, a set of teeth, a human hand and other rubber practical jokes. The other window contained an assortment of masks and some fireworks.

Had the design of the shop not led me to its windows, I would not have looked at it twice. It was incongruous that this store, with its cheap toys and tricks, was set among some of the finest antique dealers in Europe.

What made me bother to peer through the glass in the door, I don't know. Perhaps it was because the other two windows offered no hint as to what the store itself looked like, but then again, I couldn't have expected much.

The shop was badly lit and my own presence in the doorway darkened it further. A yellowish light came from somewhere inside, and I could make out several more shelves of plastic toys, masks, party hats, crepe paper and fireworks. The ceiling was obscured by low-hanging coloured cloths, papers and ornaments – bells, balls and *papier maché* objects, garishly painted.

Then, I noticed, along the walls above the shelves, below the clutter of hangings, a row of unframed pictures. They looked like tempera, or watercolours. The one I first focused on was of a werewolf, snarling with its sharp canines dripping blood. The painting, with the exception of the drops of blood, was painted entirely in black. Another painting was of a clown in bright greasepaint; another, the face of a gorilla. My eyes followed the row of pictures

The Magic Shop

around the room: bats, devils, scenes of nightmarish suggestion with distorted figures, running, screaming, dying. The picture nearest the door was a portrait of a girl with long dark hair. There was a dark mark in the middle of her forehead from which reddish paint streamed down the paper, obliterating her features.

There was another picture, directly opposite; I couldn't quite make out what it was. A colour somewhere between oxblood and sepia. From where I was standing, I liked the form of it, even though I could not discern the subject. I went in to look more closely.

Like most of the old shops I had been in that day, this one had a musty, slightly decayed smell. The wooden floor creaked as I stepped in, and the closing door set off a barrage of bells and small chimes.

Once inside, I studied the shelves, the ceiling and all the pictures. They were like posters for a *théatre des morts*, or advertisements for a waxworks. Yet, they were neither of these things: they were simply paintings someone called "Sara" had done. They were all signed and dated, either on the painting itself or on the surround board.

I examined the picture that intrigued me. It was the only abstract in the collection. It seemed to have been made from a block print that had been rolled over with the brayer several times. The shapes in the picture were varied, but to me, there was an archway, some steps and

Undivulged Crimes

a wispy figure, vaguely female, standing beneath the arch. On the mounting board was written "Sara '71."

I looked to see if the bells had brought anyone from the back of the shop. They hadn't. I peered through a small doorway, partially covered with a beaded curtain. Something moved, but I couldn't tell what. Footsteps, then a figure approached.

"Si?" said a voice simultaneously with the pushing aside of the curtain.

A girl entered. She had strikingly beautiful features, long dark hair which clung to her shoulders and piercing dark eyes. It was a shock to see someone so attractive in this very odd shop.

"Si?" she repeated tentatively.

Her voice was broad, gentle and so rich that it seemed to fill every corner of her mouth.

"Do you speak English?"

"A little," she answered.

"How much is this one?" I asked, pointing to the picture.

She walked to it, squinting to see some identifying mark.

She turned and opened a small book on a shelf behind the counter. After turning a few pages, she said:

"Cinc-cents pessetes."

"How much?"

The Magic Shop

"I'm sorry," she gave the hint of a smile. "Five hundred pesetas."

"I'd like to have it."

She said nothing, but stepped on a low stool and pulled the drawing pin from poster board and lay the picture on the counter. As I looked down at it, I noticed a small pile of flat coloured cardboard face-masks, the sort that used to come on the back of cereal boxes. Elmer Fudd, Mr Magoo, Daffy Duck and Bugs Bunny.

I wondered what sort of business the shop did. Except for the pictures, which had a fairly narrow appeal, and the fireworks, there was nothing in it which couldn't have been bought at any five and ten with foreign branches.

She wrapped the picture in tissue paper and gave it to me as I gave her the five hundred peseta note. I had little idea how much five hundred pesetas was worth, but I had a few of them in my wallet, so it couldn't be too much.

She turned to leave the room as soon as she touched the note, but I stopped her.

"Who paints these?"

She looked around the room at the grotesque collection of screams, blood and hair and said, "A girl," and disappeared into the back room.

೧

I drifted in and out of several other shops. I bought some candles in a store below Plaza San Jaime, and also visited the studio workshop of Gelpi, the sculptor and

Undivulged Crimes

printmaker who specialises in carving owls. His neat studio, near the side of the cathedral, was filled with caged birds. I bought a print and a small bronze medallion with an owl on it.

The next day, it was late afternoon when I turned into the street of the Magic Shop. When I walked into the shop, it looked the same, except a new picture hung where mine had been; a bluish figure of a girl, or the ghost of a girl. The lines were barely discernible; it had been drawn in water on a wash of pale blue.

I was staring at it when the girl walked in.

"Hello," I said.

"Do you want another picture?" she asked.

"They're fascinating. All of them." She smiled, but said nothing.

I walked from picture to picture and she watched me closely. Just up the street, the bell in the cathedral rang five times.

"I must close," she said quietly.

I didn't want to leave. I didn't want to buy anything. I wasn't even certain I liked the picture I had already purchased. It was the atmosphere; something was there and wanted knowing.

I asked if I could buy her a drink, since she was closing. She started to refuse, then hesitated.

"Not now," she said. "Eight o'clock."

I stepped outside the shop, then asked her name.

The Magic Shop

"Belén," she said carefully, then locked the door.

I waited in front of the shop at eight. The steel shutters were down and hid the façade. I had only been there a few moments when she appeared. She had come from the direction of the cathedral.

"Hola," she said with a warm smile. Her manner was more relaxed and friendly than it had been that afternoon.

"Where are we going?" she asked.

"Somewhere where there aren't any tourists."

"Impossible. If you're there, there are tourists – or at least one." Her English was excellent, with only a slight accent.

Her voice had the richness I had heard the day before. Words formed in her throat and picked up a rare depth of tone as she spoke them.

"I think I know a place you'll like. Come."

She led the way down the narrow street. By my generally good sense of direction, I felt we were headed towards the Ramblas, but after about half a mile, we must have made enough subtle turns so that we were either parallel to it, or even heading away from it.

Belén seemed to read my thoughts.

"This is a magic street. It doesn't go where you expect. It made a good place to hide during the civil war. Ah, here we are."

Undivulged Crimes

She stopped by a dark building and went up the long flight which led into a recessed doorway. She walked in. There were several groups of potted plants near the door and tables beyond them. Light fixtures hung very low over the tables so the room was dim.

She spoke to a waiter who indicated a table at the far wall. When I sat down, I had the chance to look around.

There was a large open fireplace with huge beams across it. The ceiling was dark with an ancient pattern, barely discernible, painted on it. Odd copper pots, utensils and curiously shaped iron tools hung on the wall. Above our table was a watercolour, done entirely in black, of a figure who seemed to be tied to a stake. At the lower left of the picture was pencilled the name, Sara.

We drank a pitcher of wine before deciding to stay for dinner. The Spanish menu bewildered me. I asked Belén to order.

"Are you daring when it comes to food?"

"Only if I don't know what I'm eating."

"There are some things it is better not to know."

My line had been frivolous. Hers was not. I looked at her carefully. What would bother a girl as hauntingly beautiful as Belén?

I didn't have too much time to think about it; the waiter came for the order. Once she had given it, she began to describe what she had ordered.

The Magic Shop

The meal took us a full two hours. Four courses and more wine. We mostly talked about silly things. I didn't ask about her or about the shop. She didn't ask about me.

We talked of travelling and of Spain, but only generally. Franco was still in power, and opinions were not expressed in public places, and certainly not to strangers. In Barcelona, the Catalonians could be fiercely independent.

Belén had been in most of the Mediterranean countries. She spoke freely and had a warmth which made her easy to be with.

After dinner, we walked towards the Ramblas.

"Where are you staying?" she asked.

"A cheap hotel near the university."

"We're not too far from there now, if you'd like to go from here. Or you may come for a cup of bad coffee."

Her eyes were very bright in the dark. Street lights cast shadows which made her features even more fascinating. Neon signs flashed red, blue and green patterns across her eyes and cheeks.

We walked silently through the streets, not looking in the shop windows, not paying attention to the crowds on their way from the theatres.

I felt we were very close to the street where the shop was, yet nothing looked familiar. Then we came to a doorway and Belén took out two keys. The door was up several steps from the street and recessed into the building. There was a stone arch over the steps. She unlocked the door and went in. I waited until she turned on a light.

"Come in. It's safe," she laughed.

It wasn't a very large room. There was an old sofa, a desk, two or three chairs and a drop-leaf table. In an alcove was a small gas stove and a sink with some cupboards.

"Do you know where you are?" she asked.

"No, but I feel I should be near the shop."

"Very good. The shop is through there," she said, indicating a narrow passage. "We came in from the other side."

She put the water on the stove and took two mugs from the shelf. She sat next to me on the sofa, turned so we faced each other.

"Is the shop yours?"

"It's been in my family for many years. I run it myself now."

"Did you always sell – " I stumbled, trying to find a charitable name for the merchandise.

"For generations," she said softly. "Fireworks, disguises and grotesque paintings. It would astound you how many items we have sold over the years."

"Are your customers mostly children?"

The Magic Shop

"For the little things, yes. But we attract many others, such as yourself, who for some reason are intrigued by the paintings. Why did you buy that one yesterday?"

"I don't know, it had a certain – "

"You see? You can't explain it. You don't really *like* it, do you? But it did attract you. You'll keep it forever and even defend it against people who tell you it's ugly."

She paused and gave an ironic laugh.

"What is it?"

"They will be right, too: the people who say the painting is ugly. It's a horrible picture. It's the colour of blood; it's smeared on to the paper in evil shapes."

Her expression had changed. She was reflecting the words which she spoke about the picture. Her voice was agitated.

"It's a wicked picture. They're *all* wicked pictures. Horrible. Frightening, terrible!"

I felt uncomfortable now. Perhaps I shouldn't have bought the picture. Was she attacking my taste, or did she think I had recognised it as what she described? I tried to visualise my picture as she spoke. She was right in one thing: I -would- defend it against people who attacked it.

The picture was now more than just one casually picked up on a European trip; it had a story and a person behind it.

She handed me the mug of coffee.

Undivulged Crimes

"Are you going to be in Barcelona long?" she asked. Her voice was again soft and calm.

"I don't know. Originally, I had planned to stay only a few days. Now, I am tempted to stay longer."

"It is a very old city, and there is much to see."

"Will you show it to me?"

"No."

"I could come after you close – "

"No, don't."

"Suppose I came to buy another painting?"

"Don't. They're all bad."

"Badly done or evil?"

"Both. Take the one you have, frame it in black. Hang it in your home. Enjoy it if you can, but forget about all this. Now, please go; and, thank you for dinner."

I took my coat and went to the door. On the step, I looked back at her. She was ready to close the door.

"Good night," she said gently.

I leaned towards her and quickly, but deliberately, kissed her.

"Oh, God!" she whispered sharply.

"May I see you again?"

Her silence made me feel that she didn't want to think of that possibility.

"Tomorrow night. At the same time," she said quickly and closed the door.

The Magic Shop

I stayed in Barcelona for five weeks. When I left, it was only because I had to return to work. I would like to have stayed longer, but looking back, events had run their course.

Belén took me to dinner the second night. Her mood was a little more serious, but she was very good company. We had coffee at her house and talked until very late. I was ignorant of Spanish literature, and she was widely read.

On the weekend, she took me to Sagrada Familia and to the Picasso Museum. On Sunday afternoon, she was very pleased to learn that I wasn't the least interested in seeing a bull fight.

We roamed the ancient streets and the new ones. She told me where the battles were fought in the Civil War and where the witch trials were during the Inquisition.

We went to Montjuic and rode the baskets across the harbour. We ate and drank in tapas bars and went to the theatre.

From time to time, I'd drop in to see her at the shop. Often there were new paintings to take the places of those which had been sold, but I never saw anyone else in the shop.

"Does Sara bring the paintings to the shop?" I asked.
"Yes."
"I'd like to meet her some time."
"You wouldn't like her. She's like her pictures."

Undivulged Crimes

"I'd still like to meet her."

"Maybe sometime."

I spent my days exploring the area and going to the beaches to the south. I did a lot of nothing, but filled the days with something until it was closing time at the magic shop.

One night she cooked dinner for me. We had a great deal to drink and were rather silly during dessert.

"I've grown very fond of you," I said over coffee.

"I know. It's dangerous."

"*Dangerous*? Why?"

"Because you have your own life to lead, and I have mine. You have your world, and I have mine. They have come together for a while now, but they will separate once again."

"Do you think I'm that insincere?"

"No. I think you're very close to falling in love with me. But you must not."

"Are we that different?"

"Yes. Some of us have our own private worlds as well as those we live in. Worlds which don't pay attention to time. These worlds possess one completely. I could leave my world here in Barcelona, but I could never leave my private world."

I hate it when women talk like that, but she spoke in such a way that I couldn't question it. There were barriers there which I could not overcome.

The Magic Shop

One particularly warm Saturday, we took a bus down to one of the beaches. The coming summer heat could be felt in the sun. We took a picnic and had lunch in the sunny shelter of some dry rocks.

After the meal, and a good bottle of wine, we dozed in the sunshine. It was while in a state of semi-consciousness that I became dimly aware of movement.

Belén was moving restlessly in her sleep. She was speaking softly in Spanish. Though I couldn't understand what she said, it sounded like exclamations of protest. I lifted her by the shoulders and gently tried to wake her.

Suddenly, she gave a horrifying scream and sat up with a jolt, then, coming to, took hold of me and burst into tears. I tried to comfort her, but she stood up and began to gather our things.

She was quiet on the bus back to Barcelona, but said the odd trivial thing. She did not seem disturbed.

I walked with her back to her house.

"Will you come in for coffee?" she asked.

"No, it's late – "

"Please come in." I went in.

In the sitting room, she sat looking at me.

"It's time for you to know," she said.

"Is something wrong?"

"No. It's as it should be. For me."

She paused, considering something.

"Come. It's better to show you."

Undivulged Crimes

I followed her up three ancient flights of stairs until we were on the top floor which was a great open loft. She turned on two bare lightbulbs which hung from the rafters. The room was used as a studio. Canvases and used tubes of paint were scattered everywhere. All of the pictures were grotesque; all were signed "Sara."

"You are Sara."

"Yes."

"I thought so. Why the secret?"

"Come," was all she said.

She led me down the stairs again. We turned into a set of rooms on the floor beneath the loft. She turned on more lights.

Paintings hung in ornate gilt frames, filling every available square foot of wall space. A quick survey yielded two observations about the pictures: they spanned about four hundred years of history, and they were all grotesque. All major art movements were represented from the fifteenth century to surrealism.

I walked from one to the other, amazed at the subjects, the horror, the suffering. At the far end of the long narrow room, one painting seemed to enjoy a place of prominence. It was a large canvas depicting the burning of a witch in the square before the cathedral. On the steps of the church, watching the conflagration was a gathering of priests, bishops and cardinals.

The Magic Shop

It struck me because I had only that day seen the cathedral from a similar angle and in the same light. The photographic quality of the painting added to the peculiar feeling that it was just a still from a film production. Automobiles should be there, not bales of sticks and the ominous wooden stake.

"That is the oldest painting of the collection," Belén said.

I looked directly at her, then scanned several other paintings.

"There's a story that goes with all this, isn't there?"

"Yes, there is. A story more frightening than all of the paintings."

We completed the tour of the rooms on that floor. There were more demons, vampires, ghosts and macabre scenes in academic, impressionist and primitive styles. In the last room, there were two modern pictures signed, "Sara."

Belén walked down the stairs and sat on the sofa.

"There's one good part to the story, as far as you're concerned: the picture you bought from me is a good one. It will come to be highly regarded, though perhaps not in your lifetime.

"All of the paintings you saw were done by members of my family. The first one was painted in 1564 by a direct ancestor; nearly twenty generations back. He was a cardinal and the woman tied to the stake was his mistress, the mother of the family line.

"By claiming she had seduced a man as devout as himself, he was easily able to have her convicted of witchcraft. He painted himself standing on the cathedral steps. She cursed him as the torch was set to the tinder. She is also supposed to have given him an address where his bastard son might be found.

"He ignored her, but in the weeks which followed her execution, he became troubled by dreams about her and other young women who had been persecuted. Somehow, he was moved to paint pictures of the horrors he dreamt.

"In time, he went to the address where his son was being kept and made himself known to the boy and supervised his education. This was the building. It's been in the family since then, though it is much changed.

"When the cardinal died, he was buried in the cathedral. Within a week, the son began to have dreams of the horrors of the inquisition, and then he, too, began to paint.

"And so it has been for four hundred years. I have the dreams now. I do the painting."

She paused to look at me for a reaction.

"I cannot describe the dreams," she went on. "They frighten me terribly, as you saw. They occur about once a week. I am compelled to paint. All of us were.

The Magic Shop

"People do buy the pictures and I, and my ancestors, have always prayed that the horror of the pictures will cause their owners to eliminate terror and injustice from their lives."

She took my hand.

"It's an odd and terrible thing to live with. But one day, I shall find someone who will tolerate being awakened with screaming. I shall have one child; that is the pattern; that child shall paint and dream just as I."

I didn't know whether to believe her or not. I knew I had seen the paintings. Even with this extraordinary tale, Belén remained very attractive. I told her so.

"Don't be so afraid to say so," she said with the trace of a smile. "You're not the one."

I laughed.

"How do you know?"

"Because I love you."

She held me for a moment in the chill of the sparse room. I was about to kiss her when she pulled back to look at me with those dark, haunted eyes.

"Now, leave," she whispered. "Leave - while you can."

I left the next day, my mind confused, and my spirit shaken.

I have never gone back to Barcelona, sensing it is one of those things better left undisturbed. Yet, the separation hadn't been complete, and my memories of Belén are still vivid, for I dream of her every week.

Undivulged Crimes

The Return of Colonel Thurston

The Return of Colonel Thurston

Undivulged Crimes

The Return of Colonel Thurston

Colonel Thurston didn't visit his house too often anymore. True, the bougainvillea still blossomed along the pillars and balconies and smelled as sweet as they had ever done, but, somehow, the place didn't have the appeal that it used to.

It had all been so different before the war. The plantation had been thriving and always alive with the sound of voices, singing, laughing and talking.

Reflecting on past events, he judged himself again and again, but never with regret. He had been good to his family – a loving husband and father. He had been a kind slave owner, giving his slaves decent housing and food, and he employed only honest, reasonable managers. He never chained or beat the slaves, and frequently visited them and laughed and smoked with them. Only once in fifteen years had a slave escaped, a malcontented, boy, full of abolitionist propaganda, who had taken some money from a manager and promptly spent it on drink. A friend of the colonel had found the lad lying in some wasteland in a stupor and returned him.

Colonel Thurston had said nothing, but gave him new clothes, fed him and sent him back into the fields. The boy never tried to leave again.

Undivulged Crimes

Not much of a victory, the colonel thought, but certainly an incident which he could have handled differently with more regrettable results.

But what did a runaway matter? There were no slaves anymore. The only slaves were the Southern whites. Slaves to the North, Washington and President Johnson.

The house, Longwood, had escaped the plunder which accompanied the invasion of the Union Army. His family and staff stayed there, safely, thank God, and worked as best they could.

New taxes and regulations would ruin them, and much of his fortune had gone on Confederate bonds. Still, he could offer a modest living to a few of his former slaves. He offered a home to those who were too old, or too strangely loyal to leave the plantation.

Land would have to be sold to support the house. Although the cotton fields were intact, they were badly neglected. Three years of growth had choked the plants and tangles of rotting cotton covered many acres.

Colonel Thurston had surveyed the damage when he first returned and saw that things were put in order.

His pride had nearly been broken, but he had fought the impulse to give up. Had Longwood been destroyed upon his return, he may have been beaten. Even now, his only purpose was to keep going; to make his presence felt.

Curiously, he felt no hatred toward his Yankee conquerors, only the urge to remain the Southern

The Return of Colonel Thurston

gentleman, indomitable in adversity, remained. He didn't dare to think how ineffectual this really was.

Ineffectuality was not something he dwelt on, because he was used to success; he had earned all his success. He had built Longwood; he had successfully drained the marshland and made it fertile; he had taken risks and made them come out in his favor and flourish.

In the economic struggle with the North, he had been part of the bold resistance. Its failure was a result of fate, rather than of failure of ability. He recognized this, not from vanity, but from a well-educated sense of history.

His entire family gained strength from him, and presented a genuinely united front.

The death of his son, Quentin, in the early days of the war only succeeded in closing the ranks of the family more firmly, and when he went to war himself, he felt certain that Longwood, its household and lands, would remain essentially unchanged.

Because he was not unknown in Confederate political circles, he had been commissioned a Cavalry major. As all gentlemen of his ilk, he was an expert horseman. He was also a born leader.

With the army, he had traveled north and engaged the enemy in Maryland and in Pennsylvania. He had arrived to cover the fallback after Gettysburg. He had been with General Jackson, and as a result of his strategic acumen, he had been promoted to lieutenant colonel after

Undivulged Crimes

only a year of active service.

He served under Robert E. Lee for a few months, but they were a disappointment. The great general was having a fairly easy time of it and most of the effort was in supplying relief and cover for advancing or retreating forces.

During the year 1863, Thurston had his fiftieth birthday. He was offered desk jobs and posts at relatively safe forts in the deep south. These he refused and used all the influence he had to remain as near to the front lines as he possibly could.

Within six months, every soldier was in the front lines and the entire South was a battlefield.

Colonel Thurston had been given a company of boys. Eager and inexperienced, they had moved northward, patrolling the railway and telegraph lines. They occasionally shot at a scout, a deserter or a saboteur. They took no prisoners because none came their way.

Thurston had wondered how he would treat a prisoner. He felt he hardly treated his own company well; he could scarcely treat a prisoner better. He would act the gentleman, if his prisoner were a gentleman, but he wasn't apt to capture a gentleman.

His men moved along the railway. It was exciting to see the war machinery heading north. Men, supplies, great long trains with flags of the Confederacy flying.

But there were other trains, too. Trains of the

The Return of Colonel Thurston

wounded and dying. Trains hauling scrap metal, which had been new wagons and guns the previous month; trains which carried parts of ruined railroad cars and engines lines south where someone would try to make cannon from them.

"Don't worry about that lads," he'd say. "It's a real war going on. We knew it wouldn't be easy. The Confederacy knew what it was up against and they were prepared. Wars cost."

He knew his speeches couldn't counter the effect of the long trains transporting the wounded. His men showed their youth at times and waves of homesickness swept through the company. Colonel Thurston was not unaffected either. Homesickness brings with it that insecurity of believing that nothing would ever again be as it was. It carried also that sense of foreboding, that, as if things weren't bad enough, they were soon to get worse.

From a military point of view, Colonel Thurston felt that the best thing for his company was a little successful combat. However, he was not likely to get any combat now.

Along the railways, he'd better hope he didn't get any – if he did, it would mean that a major section of the South's defenses had been routed, or embarrassingly breached. The thought was not appealing.

To keep prepared, Colonel Thurston counted the trains each day and had guards log them at night.

Undivulged Crimes

Knowing how many carriages and wagons headed north or south each day was as good as receiving a daily newspaper, and was probably more reliable.

Colonel Thurston, then, did notice the fact that there had been more south-bound than north-bound traffic. He was horrified one day when eight trains headed south and only two went north. The following day, there had been no trains at all. The men had noticed, too, and were more apprehensive than usual. He had made a joke about it being a public holiday, President Davis' birthday or wedding anniversary, but it was all very hollow.

They were now in Kentucky. He had received orders to continue along the line. Orders were received via telegraph either by tapping the lines, or through offices in small towns. They were to continue northward. Soon they would come to a town where there was an important junction on the east-west line. They would meet another company coming from the east and proceed northward with them.

It was early evening when they approached the junction. They could see the engine sheds and station buildings ahead. They wound down the roadbed through lush greenery. The slope of the line and its hugging of the hillside gave beautiful views.

The grandeur of the landscape and the prospect of meeting the other company had a bracing effect on the men. They had not minded their long, dull march; they

The Return of Colonel Thurston

had pride of purpose. However, they were unprepared for what they found a few moments later.

The gradient lessened and straightened. Their pace picked up and the town was only a mile or so ahead. They looked forward to a little relaxation.

Colonel Thurston was about two-thirds of the way back in the column talking with the captain when the men in front of him stopped. The colonel halted his horse and stood in the stirrups looking ahead. The column had come to a dead stop for no apparent reason.

He moved his horse around the men and went to the head of the company. They stood staring blankly at the roadbed.

There were no rails.

They had been neatly taken up as far as the eye could see. Not a plate or a spike was to be found. Metal signs were removed and the switch cables were also gone.

Telegraph poles were wireless.

The meaning of what they saw was not lost on them. The South, at least this part of the South, had been beaten. Union soldiers were, no doubt, in possession of the town.

The effect of the scene on the men was that curious feeling which one has at moments of personal disaster: a refusal to believe that events confronting one are really happening; the desperate hope that it is a mistake.

Colonel Thurston deliberated his next move. He had

Undivulged Crimes

been ordered to the rail head, but that now looked impossible or suicidal. He could turn south again to the next telegraph office, but that would mean leaving the road open for the Union advance; or, consulting his map, he could strike out, cross country, to join the company on the eastern line, if they had not already passed.

That course of action seemed the most sensible to the colonel. It was the most profitable and least fool-hardy. He consulted briefly with the captain, then sent a rider over the hills to find a route to the eastern railroad line, and, if possible, establish contact with the other company.

Colonel Thurston then withdrew his company up the hill out of sight of the town.

The eastern railroad line could only be four or five miles away, so the report was expected in less than two hours.

The rider was never seen again.

At four o'clock, a shot was heard by one of the sentries. The men aimed their guns, in a rather shabby fashion, but never fired, for an entire division of soldiers rose before them. A moment later, a second division appeared.

There was nothing to do but surrender.

Arms were collected and the small company was marched to the railroad station. Their horses were taken from them, except the colonel and the captain who were

The Return of Colonel Thurston

allowed to ride with two junior Union officers.

Within two hours, the company had been loaded into freight cars and sent northward. The captain had been sent too, but Colonel Thurston remained behind. He had chains on his ankles and wrists, and sat alone in the waiting room of the station. Half a dozen trains steamed in and out on the east-west line while he waited. He watched and felt alone.

At seven o'clock, a corporal came to him.

"Major Lowell presents his compliments, Colonel, and invites you to share dinner with him."

There was no need to reply. Colonel Thurston followed the corporal to what had been the station manager's office. It still looked much the same, except additional maps had been placed on the walls, and there was a cache of guns in a far corner.

"Colonel Thurston, welcome," the major said. "I'm Major George Mason Lowell. Please, sit down."

The major was a dark man with longish hair, but carefully shaved, with a fussily trimmed moustache. He had a rather brutal face, a muscular build and very cold, very blue, eyes. His manner was civilized, educated and easy.

"My men – " Colonel Thurston began, before sitting down.

"Your boys will be all right, but they will be sitting out the rest of the war. Don't worry about them, they're beyond your control now. Sit down, please."

Undivulged Crimes

A corporal came in and cleared the desk and spread a white linen table cloth and set two places. A bottle of wine was put on the table, and the major poured two glasses.

"To – " the major paused, glass in hand. "To peace."

"To peace."

The colonel drank with the major.

"You're not a military man, Colonel?"

"A plantation owner. And you?"

"A civil engineer. Harvard."

"William and Mary. Classics."

"A wonderful subject for a gentleman, but for those who have to work, engineering has to do. My interest was railroads, which is probably why I'm here."

He gestured around the office.

"A plantation owner doesn't get much time for scholarship," the colonel said. "But it does give one a view of history and an insight into human nature."

"Quite so."

Soup had arrived and the men began eating.

"Tell me, Colonel, do you really think the South will win?"

"I'm not a military man. I don't know what we've got. But if it doesn't, it will have been one of the worst wastes of lives in the history of the world."

"It's that already."

"As you say, Major. I fear that the South is much like

The Return of Colonel Thurston

Troy, and there are sparks flying in the topless towers."

A cooked duck and several dishes of vegetables were placed on the table.

"I dread the peace more than this war, if the South loses," Colonel Thurston said quietly.

"Rape and pillage?"

"Oh, there's always that. But the slaves will be free, and the entire South will be enslaved."

"That can only be temporary," the major said. "The North needs the South too much to keep it a cripple. Unfortunately, the South needs the North too much to win this war. Have some more peas."

"What do you want from this war, Major?"

"The same as you, probably; to go home. I haven't been home in over a year."

"Family?"

"A wife and son."

"I have two daughters, and my wife. My only son was killed at Pittsburg Landing."

"I am very sorry, Colonel."

"War brings its casualties."

"You mentioned Troy. Is there a parallel between this war and an ancient one?"

Colonel Thurston thought, then shook his head.

"Not really. All wars have much the same result. Regardless who wins or loses, life is never the same afterwards. Had the Trojans won, they would have become

Undivulged Crimes

corrupt and decadent. They were felled at the height of their glory, so we regard it as particularly heroic and tragic."

"And generals?" the major asked.

'They're only tragic, if they're too idealistic.'

"Macbeth idealistic?"

"He believed he was important enough to command Divine privilege."

"And other great generals?"

"Generals aren't great: they are strong or weak; intelligent or stupid and just plain lucky or unlucky. No more. The rest is myth."

Major Lowell peeled an apple.

"Are you a gambling man, Colonel."

"Only occasionally. I don't bet anything I can't afford to lose."

"You're a careful man. I rather think that only betting things you can't afford to lose are worth betting. The other sort of betting is idleness at its worst. But that isn't criticism of you, Colonel, merely the way I see things."

"Isn't that rather reckless betting, Major?"

The major looked over his apple peeling. He was an intense man. It showed even in his concentration as an apple peeler.

"No. Big risks for big gains, little risks for little gains. I just don't bother with little gains. Do you play chess, Colonel?"

The Return of Colonel Thurston

"Yes, Major."

"What say you to a game, then. I'll even place a good bet on it. One which should interest you."

They finished the fruit. The corporal cleared the table. The major brought a chess set out of the desk. He also brought out a bottle of whisky and two glasses.

The colonel drew black.

They set up the board and each made two moves.

"Ah, the wager," Major Lowell said.

"Go on, Major."

"I'll gamble your freedom."

"I beg your pardon, sir?"

"If you win this game – just this one – I'll give you your freedom. That's it – you see, I can't really afford to lose you. I have a colonel, too, you know."

"What's in the bet for you if I lose?"

"I keep you. Perhaps it doesn't seem like much, but it's a darn sight better than losing you, which I can't afford to do."

He poured the whiskey.

"Do we have a bet?"

"Major, I have everything to lose and everything to gain. In effect, I'd be playing with no pressure on me at all. It's hardly fair."

The major scrutinized him.

"Colonel, just you try to believe that."

They drank agreement to the wager.

Undivulged Crimes

With each piece he played, Colonel Thurston felt the thread of his life stretched or twisted. Each lost piece was like losing a friend. He chided himself for regarding the pawns as his slaves.

The game was slow. The candles burned without movement, and the level of the bottle slowly fell. Neither player took his eyes from the board. Their gentlemanly honor did not extend to refraining from trying to split the pieces, or trying to change a bishop into a rook.

The pieces began to fall after a long period of moving about, avoiding confrontation; not calling bluffs. Inevitably, the pace picked up. Pawns were sacrificed, knights exchanged, bishops risked and queens finessed, then quickly moved from danger.

The rhythm of the game subsided again. It became ponderous, an endurance test: will, strength, stamina, a very civil war.

The victory was revealed, not won. It became apparent, not suddenly by blunder or master stroke, but gradually. Colonel Thurston had the advantage. He played carefully, seeming not to notice that the major had become defensive.

Even in the closing moves, the major made no errors, no desperate bluffs or sacrifices; he merely continued his movement until the colonel spoke.

"Checkmate."

Major Lowell looked at the board for a last moment,

The Return of Colonel Thurston

then reached for the bottle. He refilled, both glasses.

"Congratulations, Colonel. The best game I've had all war."

They drank.

Then the major opened his desk and drew out a large ring of keys. He walked around to Colonel Thurston and knelt beside him and unfastened his leg irons.

He took the colonel's hat from a peg, and also lifted down the officer's sword and cape, and took them to him.

"You will understand if I don't give you a gun."

"Certainly."

The major walked back behind his desk. The colonel stood and buckled on his sword. Major Lowell saluted him, and the salute was returned.

"I give you your freedom, Colonel," he said, and saluted.

"Good night, Major," the colonel replied, returning the salute.

Colonel Thurston turned smartly and walked out of the office.

Major Lowell poured himself another drink and went to the window. The colonel was crossing the road.

One shot split the silence, and Colonel Thurston fell into the dust. The major lifted his glass to the colonel's body.

"You're free, Colonel. Free to go home."

꙳

Undivulged Crimes

The bougainvillea blossomed at Longwood, and it smelled as sweet as it had ever done.

Colonel Thurston slowly descended the stairs to the front hall.

Longwood looked good; his wife and daughters looked healthy. The house was in remarkable condition considering the years of war and the lack of staff.

It was good to preside over Longwood again, and see the familiar faces of his family, friends and servants.

He just wished that they wouldn't scream so when they came upon him walking through the house.

Nick Carraway's Journal

Nick Carraway's Journal

edited by Jay & Daisy Carraway

Undivulged Crimes

Nick Carraway's Journal

Nick Carraway's Journal

I had no idea that Dad was keeping a journal. I didn't discover it until after he died, and it has left us with more questions than answers.

My sister, Daisy, and I had picked up a few things over the years, but they were merely unconnected dots and we never had much of an idea of what the whole picture was.

Looking over these pages now, I see that I have written more than Dad did. I hope it helps. Daisy has written quite a few pages of this, too, but doesn't want to confuse things by shifting back and forth too much.

Why don't I start with who I am what I knew of my father. Perhaps then it will help readers to understand our surprise at learning what we did about Dad. About our mother, too, as she was still alive when we started on this project eight years ago.

This is the information we grew up with about Dad:

Nicholas Madison Carraway was born Minneapolis, Minnesota, in 1894, the only son of Henry (Harry) Carraway and Martha Madison. He had a sister, Eleanor (Ellie) who was three years younger. She, too, lived to a ripe old age, dying only a year before Dad, in 1990.

My grandfather had gone to Yale, class of 1890, and Dad followed him, graduating in 1915, just in time to see

Undivulged Crimes

some of the action of the "Great War," as he always called it. I understand the British still do. Dad served as an ordinary soldier in the First Division ("Big Red One"), 28th Infantry. The unit saw action at a string of campaigns: Montdider-Noyon, Aisne-Marne, St Mihiel, Meuse-Argonne (Battle of the Argonne Forest), Lorraine and Picardy.

I never heard him talk about the war, and it's not mentioned in any of his journal entries. He didn't keep his uniform, campaign ribbons, or any souvenirs at all. From what I can make out, it was the only time he went to Europe.

When he got back from the war, his father was still doing well in the hardware business. From all I've heard, he got on well with his father, and they had an understanding that Dad needed to build his own life, just to see if he could, before returning to the mid-west and learning how to sell hardware.

It's hardly surprising that he went to New York. It was where the post-war action was. The moneymaking, the music, the action.

I don't know how his degree from Yale made him qualified to sell bonds at the Probity Trust. Most likely, there was a guy from Yale working there who arranged for him to be hired. He was there for six or seven years before returning to Minneapolis in late 1925. I used to

Nick Carraway's Journal

think that he had some premonition about the coming crash, but his journal gives the real reason.

There are some things here that are rather difficult for children to talk about in terms of their parents. These are the, mostly casual, relationships that he seems to have had with various women while in New York. The morality then seems to have been as free-and-easy as those today, but without the threat of AIDS, or the benefits of reliable birth control. The crowd he fell in with was certainly not bothered by the conventions their parents had observed.

I have read this in English literature, too. It seems to have been a result of a normal reaction to the Victorian period, the horrors of the war and having lost so many family and friends, and the sudden affluence. After all, it had been the war to end all wars, so there was nothing to worry about. My sister and I have discussed this a lot and been forced to conclude that Mom was similar in her behavior, if not more so, as she was a less reticent person than Dad.

We nearly threw Dad's journal away because we didn't recognize it for what it was. It wasn't in a diary or bound notebook, but in a file folder comprising typed sheets. The accuracy of some of the dating suggests that he had a diary, or at least an *agenda* which he referred to, but the entries appear to be a combination of passages that were written at the time, and those that were added in retrospect. All the pages appear to have been typed on

Undivulged Crimes

the family typewriter, which dates from the time of Dad's return to Minneapolis.

We had heard about the Gatsby murders – every one of our generation grew up with our parents' stories about what the world was like before the crash; how people entertained, had dozens of staff, and great houses that were run like principalities. Gatsby's life – or at least some of it – was well known, and better known was his love for an elusive, and ultimately unworthy woman, and how it led to his destruction. Gatsby stories were the fairy tales of our childhood, like the moral fable of the death of Calvin Coolidge's son, Lindbergh's flight or the court martial of Billy Mitchell.

It never occurred to us that when Mom and Dad spoke of Gatsby and his circle that they were speaking from first-hand knowledge.

This account is mostly for ourselves, our children, and friends who have expressed an interest in these vignettes from the jazz age.

CB

The Yale Club
New York

September 22, 1920

I thought that after the war, few things would surprise me. The size, noise and bustle of New York City was something I didn't expect. It is

Nick Carraway's Journal

almost as noisy and chaotic as the war, but it's the chaos of life, not death. There is music everywhere, in restaurants, in the streets, and pouring from the windows of tenements from ten thousand radios on every block.

Financial institutions aren't noted for their noise, but in the large open office where I work, there is the clamor of telephones--as impossible to ignore as a howling baby. Voices rise and fall depending on the quality of the connection, or the value of the deal, while dozens of typewriters drone like mechanical cicadas. Ceiling fans squeaked, doors and dividing gates flapped back and forth, each with its unique sound, and girls at adding machines pulled handles and tore off ribbons of paper as the ticker-tape machines stuttered out gains and losses. As of yet, I am contributing little to the cacophony. I have no natural gift for conversation, but say only what needs to be said to get the job done. I don't think I was particularly quiet as a child, or at Yale. Perhaps this, too, is a result of war, when it could be impossible to speak above the noise, or to think of anything worth saying when it had stopped.

Thank goodness for the Yale Club with its civilized dining room, bar and bedrooms. I must enjoy it while I can, for I can only afford it for a few days before I will move into my monk-like cell.

First day at the office. I suppose the people are nice enough but they had little interest in a newcomer. Still, I have my own desk, telephone, swivel chair with arms, green-

Undivulged Crimes

shaded desk lamp, filing cabinet (well, a drawer in one) and periodic access to an office boy and stenographer from the pool.

Bond selling appears to be a rather curious business. People are buying and selling all day, but no real money ever seems to change hands, just numbers in columns. It's pretty daunting for someone who doesn't know anyone in this city.

Not completely true. I met Joe Rigby tonight in the bar. He was in my class and did his bit in the war with the Navy. He's living here for the next week or so. He lost his job and was kicked out of his apartment; maybe not in that order; and is either waiting for something to turn up, or for his parents to send him the train fare back to Cleveland.

At present, I'm enjoying the independence. I haven't been here long enough to be lonely, and the discovery of the city is enough to entertain me. Just like in the army, I know I'll meet a number of kindred souls and enjoy life in a modest way.

November 30, 1920

Well, things did pick up which is why I've not written anything since coming to town. Life has something of a rhythm now. I have a small apartment on Chrystie Street and appear to be surrounded by Chinese, but the apartment is clean, dry, reasonably safe and convenient to work. I walk to work when the weather permits, and even say good morning to a few people along the way.

Nick Carraway's Journal

The work is settling into a routine. I'm still learning, but it's not all that hard as long as you pay attention to what you're doing. I'm getting to know people, too. I go to lunch with a handful of different fellows. Crowded places with good sandwiches, soup and fish chowder on Friday. I eat at the Yale Club one night a week--I'm going on different nights to see if I run into people who cusped with me, but on the whole, the clientele looks more like it was at Yale when my father was.

Bunsen was there last night. He was a year ahead of me and has become a lawyer. He said he was doing well, but I had the impression he didn't enjoy it much.

What did one have to do to enjoy things? I wondered. I had the satisfaction that I was making my own way in New York City. I had a place of my own and a job that kept me busy, but apart from trying to build a routine that filled time, life is, in reality, pretty empty.

July 15, 1922

Chrystie Street
Several of us drove up to Harlem last night after dinner at the Yale Club. It's been relentlessly hot with buildings, roads, sidewalks and everything radiating heat twenty-four hours a day. The office has been so hot and airless--despite all the windows being open and the fans running--that three girls fainted today.

Undivulged Crimes

The story is that only one fainted and the other two saw the chance of getting a head start on the weekend and headed off to Atlantic City as soon as they were out of the building.

Anyway, Harlem. It was my first trip up there and I had little idea what to expect. It was safe enough, and we found the club (I think it was called the Hottentot, but the neon sign was not working) and it filled the basements of several buildings, meandering along from room to room. But in the center were the band and a small dance floor surrounded with dozens of tables.

Within minutes my eyes stung from the smoke and my shirt was soaked from the heat, but the band played with a vigor that suggested it was only sixty-five degrees.

Few people danced, but several girls in brightly colored short dresses, feathers and beads entertained the room so well that I first supposed they were part of an act.

"They're just working girls out for a good time," said Bunsen. "The one on the right is Georgia Williams."

I nodded sagely, then said:

"Should I know the name?"

"No," Bunsen said. "I know her because she's from Stamford. I used to play football with her brother. She works at an insurance office in town."

Nick Carraway's Journal

I tried to imagine the women in my office dressed like that and dancing as though their lives depended on keeping in motion. I couldn't.

When the song ended, Bunsen waved to Georgia and the three of them came to our table. Chairs were found and more glasses and drinks arrived.

"It's too hot to make a fool of one's self," said the dark-haired girl who sat next to me. "But that doesn't mean I won't try!" she added, gulping whatever was in the glass at her place, then laughing.

It was as though I had passed into a different country, a different world. The music, the costumes, the girls--these were all unknown to my life back in the city. But, in Harlem, things were sure different.

*

October 24, 1948 - A Retrospective Note[1]

The dark-haired girl called herself Ridley LaSalle, which I didn't believe was her real name for a minute, but that's what everyone called her and that's what I called her for

---

[1] Dad stuck in pages with comments on his notes, or more frustratingly, summaries of his original writing

nearly two years of an on-again, off-again affair of convenience. My notes from the time[2]

Undivulged Crimes

record only what we did together, not the weeks when we never saw each other at all. It was enough for me at the time and we didn't ask each other too many questions. Being together meant we weren't lonely for a while and neither of us was looking for anything serious or permanent.

Ridley would telephone the office and tell me to meet her at some club, apartment house, station, or once, on the pier of the Staten Island ferry. We'd find a party, drink and dance and then, one day, she was gone. She telephoned me from Pennsylvania Station and told me she had to leave New York and she was going home.

"It's a place I hope you never have to go to, but it's where I'm from, and where I'm going, and where I'll probably grow old, because it's safe."

So the girl whose real name I never knew went home to a town I didn't know where. She told me to keep whatever she left in my apartment. There wasn't much: some cheap make-up, a hairbrush and some hairpins, and a pair of rhinestone earrings. There was also a silly comb with an inverted crescent moon decorated with rhinestones and several white feathers coming out of it. She used to wear it to parties and left it here one night. I gave it to Bunsen who gave it to Georgia who wore it to a few parties.

---

[2] Lost

I threw the other things away, but put the earrings into my stud box and forgot about them.

Nick Carraway's Journal

❦

Those earrings stayed there until one day shortly after the end of WWII when Daisy and I were teenagers, Mom was helping Dad get ready for a big Christmas party and poked around in his stud box for his cuff-links and pulled out an earring.

Apparently, Mom knew about Ridley, but not about the earrings. It was completely believable that Dad had forgotten about them and didn't even see them on the occasions he opened the box. In the 1930s, in the hardware business the call for wearing gold cuff-links or tie pins wasn't great.

Mom found the other and looked at them and rather liked them, but noticed the fastening screw on one of them was missing – probably the reason they got left at Dad's apartment in the first place. He said she could have them if she wanted them, and she took them to be repaired.

When she collected them, the jeweler asked if they were family pieces, which puzzled Mom. He then told her that they were one and a half-carat diamonds, but he hadn't yet done the repair as he had to order the platinum screw. Mom told him not to bother, and took the earrings home.

She told Dad and said that Ridley must have been someone's kept woman, as she obviously didn't come from money. She said the earrings were "wages of sin"

Undivulged Crimes

(which sent Daisy and me into fits of laughter), and regardless how wicked Mom had been in her youth, she wouldn't wear them.

We found them again in the stud box after Dad died. They'd been in that box for seventy-five years apart from their brief outing to the jeweler. One day, Daisy and I will have to decide what to do with them.

ಲ

November 1924

Chrystie Street

What a notable diarist I am! Is this a sign of an uninteresting life, or a life so full of events there is no time to record it? A future biographer could do a fair job of reconstructing my life from my checkbook and bank statements.

This is my last night at Chrystie Street as I have found a house to lease. It's a small cottage on the water out on the island in West Egg. Actually, I didn't find it. Markowitz did. He works at the Probity Trust, too, but in the real estate department. That's how he heard about the bungalow. We motored to the island one Saturday and found it sandwiched between two Beaux-arts palaces, and looking very shabby, indeed. Still, it had a large lawn that reached down to the water, a comfortable porch and it wasn't far from the station if I didn't want to drive.

"Do you suppose it was a guest house or servants' residence for one of the big houses?" I asked Markowitz.

Nick Carraway's Journal

He shook his head.

"It's older than both of them," he said. "It probably belonged to some grumpy old man who didn't want to sell it to the developer."

We signed the papers and set a date to move down. I had boxes filled and a trunk packed when Markowitz came to Chrystie Street one evening shortly before we were due to move. He'd never been here and it was untidy, particularly hot, and noisy.

"I can see why you want to leave here," he said.

It had been home for four years, and I'd been happy enough, but I agreed that a home by the water would be nicer.

"Bad news, Nick. I got orders today," he said, before sitting down. "They want me to go to Washington."

"For good?"

"Well, I don't know how good it is. The guy I'm replacing just had a heart attack."

Markowitz gave me his share of two months' rent to give me a chance to make other arrangements, or to help me save enough to have the place to myself. A place of my own on the sound with grand houses as neighbors did a lot to cheer my spirits. So, on my own, I made the move, never suspecting that decision's place in the chain of events would stretch until my departure from the East.

Undivulged Crimes

༒

Dad's version of his move to West Egg doesn't quite match the better-known version, but as he said, "How could I immediately rent a house with a fellow from the office before I'd even started work and made friends with anyone?" He made the excuse that the lack of detail was because the real story wasn't about him.

༒

June 1925

West Egg

The arrival of warmer weather was welcome because even with the heating, the cottage was drafty and poorly insulated (if at all). Still, my life progressed smoother than some of my acquaintance who found themselves in some difficulty or another either with the wrong sort of woman, the wrong sort of man, or the wrong sort of gin. One of Bunsen's friends went blind for a month after a party in Atlantic City.

"That didn't stop him from driving back to New York," Bunsen added.

Around the end of April, lights began to appear in the elaborate chateau on one side of my cottage and I got to know the staff and owners. The family was the remnant of a railroad dynasty that had developed and operated a thirty-mile line that connected the city with some Connecticut towns that became fashionable because of that connection. The line was bought or leased by the New York Central or the New York, New Haven and Hartford--possibly

Nick Carraway's Journal

both, given the way of railroads at the time.

Mr. and Mrs. James Drewson II were in their mid-seventies. They lived in the city apart from the summer months, moving to "Seacliff" in early-to-mid-May and leaving by mid-September. They had three children. James Drewson III was a successful industrialist near Baltimore. He visited from time to time. In his early-forties, he had all the hallmarks of a busy, successful man. He was pleasant enough, and we played tennis a few times on their clay court, but we had little in common. His visits were short, but he and his parents clearly enjoyed each other's company. There was a daughter in her mid-thirties who lived out in Chicago with her husband and several children. They also visited each summer for a few weeks, and Mr. and Mrs. Drewson ceased all social activities while they were there. Their youngest daughter, Pamela, was just the wrong side of thirty. I suspected that both she and her mother had their eyes on me, for when Pamela was around, I was invited to enjoy generous amounts of Drewson hospitality.

Pamela was a clothes designer. Her work was bought by leading department stores and sold under their own names. She was successful, though I don't think it paid much but she drove her own Duesenberg convertible and always looked like she stepped from a magazine advertisement.

Pamela was a problem girl for both her mother and for me--at least for a while. Mrs. Drewson was very eager for Pamela to get married and I was a reasonably acceptable fellow, a Yale man

Undivulged Crimes

and not without prospects, though I would probably never run a railroad. I filled the role of extra man to make up the numbers at an embarrassing number of Drewson social and family events, and Mrs. Drewson began too many sentences with, "Pamela, why don't you show Mr. Carraway the--." You can fill in the blank with a long selection of Drewson assets: conservatory, music room, billiards room, loggia, swimming pool, picture gallery, croquet lawn, stables, beach, dock, boat.

Pamela would dutifully take me by the hand and lead me to whatever destination her mother had selected. I would make appropriate comments of appreciation, and Pamela would laugh.

It was a secret ritual we acted out when together.

The first time Mrs. Drewson had made one of her suggestions, we went to their beautiful rose garden. Both Mr. and Mrs. Drewson worked in it and Pamela told me that it was one of the places that the gardeners didn't touch while the Drewsons were in residence. She also told me that I was a good sport and that she was not as eager to find a match as her mother. Her career was prospering and that's where her interests lay. However, if I didn't find her company objectionable, she suggested we might enjoy ourselves when she was around.

We became those unusual things for a man and a woman: friends.

*

Nick Carraway's Journal

October 1978--A Retrospective Note

Pamela and I did things together on most weekends. Sometimes she brought friends from the city and didn't need my diversion. She was an excellent sailor, a good tennis player, and a witty conversationalist. Unlike her friends--and, admittedly, most of mine, who hadn't read a book since leaving college-- Pamela read voraciously: newspapers, magazines and books. She was the first person I knew who had read more than short stories by the young writers of the Great War. I had read A Farewell to Arms, and was surprised to find Pamela had, too.

She even knew several of the writers, and it was, of course, one Midwesterner in particular who, with his occasionally delightful and more often difficult, wife, was attracted by Pamela's crowd and money, and witnessed the events which he wrote about with such success.

Seacliff was the venue of several good parties that summer. Some were given by Pamela, others by her parents.

It was around mid-June when the parties at the house on the other side of me began. The ones at Gatsby's were louder, brighter, longer and frequented by less responsible people than those at the Drewsons'. The Drewsons' parties were for their friends: Gatsby's were for all the desperate moths, blinded by glamor and light. His parties were designed to attract them, and one little moth in particular: my poor cousin, Daisy.

Undivulged Crimes

Well, "poor" is the wrong word for Daisy, but after it all, I always think of her as "poor Daisy."

It's interesting to see how a writer uses reality in his fiction. Having witnessed many of the same events, the fictional treatment is like watching how films were made. I'd seen that a number of times in New York, and had always been surprised by how it looked on screen. Both fiction and films change the focus of things. In life, in a real setting, there are many things to focus on; to see, to listen to, to smell. In a book or a film, the choice of what to pay attention to has been made for you, and there is nothing else to distract you from that one thing.

The book had Tom Buchanan recreated perfectly. Self-centered and self-absorbed; not particularly good at anything, but unquestioning in the belief that he was a gentleman of many accomplishments. That's all there perfectly.

I'm drawn fairly accurately but won't admit to being quite as ineffectual.

Jordan Baker is a fabrication; a novelist's creation of a foil for Daisy, and someone for me to talk to while the others are doing the important things. In reality, the space occupied by Jordan was mostly filled by Pamela, supplemented by other women I didn't know who just showed up. Pamela and I did go to several of Gatsby's parties, so there is passing verisimilitude, but Pamela had none of Jordan's meanness.

Nick Carraway's Journal

Gatsby, like Tom, was perfectly observed and drawn. He had a charm that was unique. He did well all those things that Tom thought he did well. Next to Gatsby, Tom was an oaf.

When the film came out not long ago, I went to see it with ultimately justifiable misgivings, yet it captured the essence of Gatsby, and of Tom. Robert Redford had the boyish openness of Gatsby, but he didn't have the menace that Gatsby could have, too. That wasn't in the novel, either, so it wouldn't be in the film, but it was there in life. Gatsby could shut down like a set of Venetian blinds; all light would suddenly be gone and there would be a chill in the room as if it had suddenly become haunted. No one who experienced this wanted to remain another moment.

No one I knew ever saw Gatsby do anything violent or heard him say anything mean, but he shut people out of his life more completely than anyone, and that to some people felt like cruelty.

The only person he was ever completely open to, as far as I knew, was Daisy.

Over the years, I've given much thought to the relationship between Gatsby and Daisy. I expect many people have spent hours, writing essays and reviews, trying to make sense of them.

I have no special knowledge. Daisy was nearly six years younger than I. She was born in 1899 in Louisville. So, five years older and living in Minneapolis, we did not see each other

Undivulged Crimes

often, though there were enough family weddings, funerals and major birthdays and anniversaries that we were aware of each other and, for a while, looked forward to seeing each other. But, whether we kissed when we met or not, I do not remember, but we were not close, the proof of which was that it was from Pamela that I learned of Daisy and Tom's arrival on Long Island.

I would have expected the news to come from one of the occasional notes I received from my father giving the status of the hardware business; from someone at the Yale Club who might have seen or heard from Tom, or even from Tom and Daisy themselves. The last was, in truth, the least likely eventuality, given the way they ran their lives. It was, therefore, more than a surprise when Pamela came to my cottage one Friday evening in June and said, "I heard about a cousin of yours at Bonwit-Teller this week."

I have more than one cousin, and believed Tom and Daisy still to be in Europe, so my reply was off-hand.

"Oh, yes? Who?"

I gave Pamela a martini and sat with her on the porch swing.

"I went shopping --Tuesday, I think--and ran into Faustina O'Brien at Bonwit's."

Pamela's reports of her activities were full of detail, but because I didn't know anyone that she did, the names washed over me without

Nick Carraway's Journal

making any impact. I remembered this name from some previous narrative because it had struck me as particularly incongruous.

"I was shopping because I was bored," Pamela confessed, "but Faustina was there with someone looking for something smart for a party tomorrow night in East Egg. "At the Baker-Perkins'?" I asked. 'No, at the Buchanans'. They're just back from Europe and having a huge party. Well, I'd heard about Tom Buchanan and the string of polo ponies he took to Yale with him, and I'd heard from some Yale men about your connection with his wife. Dolly, isn't it?"

"Daisy," I said, with the curious sensation of receiving family news from strangers.

"Are you going to the party?" Pamela asked with more than a hint that I should take her, too.

"I haven't been invited," I said. "I didn't know they were back."

Pamela took this news well. She said she'd had a long week and was tired anyway. She invited me to a simple supper at her parents, served on the terrace by a butler and two maids. She then invited herself back to my house to sit on the porch, drink a cold bottle of French white wine, watch the night fall on the sound and listen to the music at Gatsby's party.

For all her cleverness, society friends and money, Pamela always seemed perfectly content and at peace on my swing, hardly talking, with my arm around her.

Undivulged Crimes

The same sort of peace did not appear to visit West Egg. Faustina O'Brien came to Seacliff the next afternoon to report on the party, and Pamela brought her over so she could tell us both--but not before Gatsby called around to ask me if I would invite Daisy for tea.

I must have told of the incident of the tea in great detail because in the book --and film-- apart from no one looking as they did and the bungalow looking nothing like it did (inside or out)--it relates it exactly as it happened.

Gatsby had just left when Pamela and Faustina arrived. I was still dazzled by his charm and presence, and puzzled by his request.

Pamela was followed by a butler with a hamper who proceeded to decorate my table with sandwiches and cakes, a bottle of wine and several shakers of various cocktails.

Pamela helped herself to a sandwich as soon as the butler left and told Faustina to tell the story.

I was wary of Faustina simply because she was part of a carefree--and careless --party crowd that moved like a plague of locusts, devouring everything when they found a place to land. Nonetheless, she was very attractive, bubbly without being silly, and had a voice that enchanted me the moment I heard it.

We passed a somnolent afternoon, drinking, talking, dozing in the heat, drinking some more and gazing at the water in silence.

Nick Carraway's Journal

During a period of our more active conversations, Faustina described the party at Daisy and Tom's.

"You couldn't really call it a party," she said. "It was more like two parties. One was Daisy's and one was Tom's. There were completely different people at each party, and things went well enough as long as they kept their distance. But, like fated ocean liners, each grand in its own way, they were destined to collide."

"There wasn't violence, was there?" Pamela asked with genuine distaste.

"It was that the people at Daisy's party liked Daisy, and those at Tom's liked Tom; the trouble was that those at Daisy's loathed Tom, and those at Tom's couldn't abide Daisy, and all of them knew about Tom's girlfriend in New York, but no one knew her name or much about her. Tom's friends had sympathy for him because Daisy had supposedly been behaving oddly since her daughter was born--which probably means that Tom wasn't getting the attention he was used to."

Faustina's comments appear to be the foundation of the character Daisy in the story. Gatsby--the real Gatsby, not the fictional one--would never have put up with the fictional Daisy. It is another of the novelist's constructs that has the fictional Gatsby so intent on recreating the past that he doesn't see Daisy clearly.

My cousin was definitely bruised by the years

Undivulged Crimes

of living with Tom, but she was still very much in control of her life. She had her own friends and activities, and was strong enough-- and rich enough on her own--not to let Tom run or ruin her.

In short, the novelist's Daisy wasn't a portrait of my cousin, but rather of his own wife.

While the essence of the plot of the relation- ship between Daisy and Tom, and Daisy and Gatsby was correct, just as the dark side of Gatsby had been glossed over, so was the strength of Daisy. She was not only determined, but more clever than the spoilt, silly Southern belle portrayed in the book. Daisy had full knowledge of Tom's infidelities and defended her position in his house vigorously, especially after the birth of their daughter. She was in a good position, too, as without her support, Tom couldn't afford the life he was leading.

No pushover, Daisy controlled her own money and only spent it on things she wanted to spend it on. She paid the lease and the servants, but Tom had to pay for his own indulgences: second, third and fourth cars, club memberships, polo ponies, grooms and stable expenses, the yacht, and bootleg alcohol.

Daisy told me this one afternoon while she waited at my house to see Gatsby. She told me she knew about Myrtle Wilson, and even knew that I had gone with them into New York to their love nest. She didn't blame me; Daisy had a generous nature.

Nick Carraway's Journal

"You didn't know what you were getting into," she said.

That was certainly true--and that was another thing that didn't come across in the book: the squalidness of Tom and Gatsby's vices. Wilson's garage was well depicted in the film, but Tom and Myrtle's apartment was not in a good neighborhood, nor was it a good building. It was a fifth-floor walk-up. No doorman, and the steady noise of families and cheap music.

*

I never felt comfortable at Gatsby's parties though Pamela and I went to a number of them that summer. As it said in the book, Gatsby seldom appeared.

While the food and music were good, the crowd was a motley, evenly split between those who were invited and those who were not. For more than a few, these parties would provide the only real meal they'd have all week.

These were relatively minor differences in the Tom-Daisy-Gatsby story, but I think a stronger Daisy would have yielded a much better story, though it didn't do badly as it was.

While I understood the relationship between Tom and Daisy pretty well, I never got to the bottom of Gatsby and Daisy. It was thick with clichés: poor adoring boy; rich, fickle girl; but Daisy wasn't that fickle or superficial. Daisy, drunk in the bath with a melting letter from Jay Gatsby makes a wonderful scene, but it requires someone much more feeble than the

Undivulged Crimes

Daisy I knew to play it. The simple fact is that, young officer or not, Jay Gatsby, poor boy, would never have gotten close enough to Daisy for her to ever really notice him. That sounds cruel, but that's the way things were in Louisville.

Jay Gatsby wasn't a southerner, so he was a foreigner. He wouldn't have known how to behave the way Daisy expected, so she never would have had the opportunity to know him. Yet, she did, and was obviously fond of him. I've often thought that Gatsby's reality--whatever it was--was so dreadful that he retreated to a gentle fantasy world of the pre-1916 South.

Curiously, it was not a time that Daisy pined for. She was intelligent enough to know that all the Tallulahs, Zeldas and Lulamays were diverted with the rituals of parties, dances, endless clothes and pampering because their parents had already chosen a husband for them. The ritual was simply to let these proud daughters of the South arrive at the same conclusion their parents did. Daisy told me she had worked this out by the time she was fourteen, but didn't tell her friends because "it would be like destroying the myth of Santa Claus or sex."

"Some of my friends still haven't caught on, and they've been married for years!" she told me.

It is true that there was nothing left to chance in the courtship of a girl of that period, location and class. The other suitors and the parade of gentlemen callers were part of a

Nick Carraway's Journal

sideshow meant for second and third daughters, or less well-off cousins.

"Being part of the nubility was a very doubtful honor," Daisy said. "It's a good thing I found Tom attractive, isn't it?"

"Have you always been so calculating?" I asked, honestly shocked by this lack of romance.

"Oh, don't feel sorry for me, Nick," she replied with a quick smile. "Tom was attractive in a lot of ways. One of them was that I knew I could control him enough to make it worth it."

Knowing what I did about Tom and Daisy by the time I had this conversation, I was surprised by the cynicism with which she accepted her life.

"It's not about me anymore," she said. "It's about little Pammy."

Confusingly, Daisy and Tom's daughter was called Pamela, which is another reason why Pamela Drewson turned into Jordan Baker in the book.

"She deserves a good home and education, and I can give her both things. It's a small price to pay in today's world," she said.

This was a long way from the Daisy in the novel saying she wanted her daughter to be a silly little girl. On the contrary, she wanted her to be clever and able to run her own life the way her mother almost could.

Undivulged Crimes

"The hardest thing is not to spoil her," Daisy said. "I can always tell when Tom's feeling particularly guilty because he buys something unneeded and very expensive for Pammy. It's one of the only things we bother to argue about anymore. She will be spoiled enough by our houses and servants and travel, but even now I tell her that the house isn't ours, we are just renting it. But, Nick, I want her to have a home. One place where she can grow up, have friends and be secure. At the moment, it looks like boarding school is the only place she'll find that, but I'll be so lonely."

It was one of those rare conversations when you feel you have really been close to someone; understood how they felt, and had a glimpse of their life and how they see the world.

Gatsby came in just after we had fallen silent and were feeling close, although physically across the porch from each other.

It was that afternoon that Gatsby gave us a tour of his house. He told us it was by McKim, Mead and White, but even then I had my doubts. Later research proved my instinct correct. Still, Daisy didn't care. Gatsby amused her, but she didn't believe everything he told her.

This was the afternoon when Daisy purportedly cried over Gatsby's shirts. Another invented scene—and ultimately cinematic—but not even Gatsby was crass enough to throw open his wardrobes in that fashion. Passing through a bedroom, he opened a closet door randomly and commented on the beautiful fittings, but it was in admiration of the house, not of his

Nick Carraway's Journal

clothing. That particular closet held some sheets and blankets, but nothing else.

Back at my house, Daisy had another drink.

"I'm glad you came along, Nick," she said. "I don't want to be alone with him. Partly because I don't fully trust him, because I don't really know him, but mostly because I don't want to give Tom the shred of a reason to suspect me of disloyalty."

"But he's--"

"Yes, he has," Daisy answered sharply. "But that doesn't make it right for me to do the same."

ೞ

Knowing what we did about the Gatsby murders, finding family links to these forgotten-world characters from that fast and loose period relatively late in life was a serious shock to our identity. My sister, Daisy, and I had never for a moment thought that we had any connection (gonnegtion) with those notorious crimes. We were only just coming to terms with our names! To our knowledge, no one pointed at us on the playground and said, "That's Daisy Carraway. Her cousin was a murderer and she's named after her."

It was a subject we had never discussed when we were growing up, but then, the war was the main topic of conversation, and stories of bootleggers and scandals from the roaring twenties were ancient history. While

Undivulged Crimes

assembling Dad's notes we were determined to read them in order, and our curiosity about what happened to Tom, Daisy, Pammy and Pamela Drewson grew. We even speculated on the more minor characters like Klippsinger, Meyer Wolfsheim, Ridley LaSalle and the endless party-goers. Golden girls all come to dust, we supposed.

The other thing that began to intrigue us was how Dad's life had such distinct sections: Youth and college; the horrors of the Great War; jazz age New York, and midwestern married life as an invisible but ultimately successful businessman. Had all the others disappeared back into innocuous and anonymous lives in the hinterlands of America?

After such an exciting start to his life, how was he able simply to leave it all in late 1925 and move to Minneapolis to sell hardware? He never again went to the parties of the rich, and even when wealthy himself, we lived in the same house and never gave more than a large Christmas party for close friends and colleagues.

ଓ

March 1928
Since moving back home, I wanted to write something more of that last summer in New York. Until now, the bitter-sweetness of it all made it too hard to be objective, and I know that I'll never be able to be fully objective about that time, those people.

My personal life was cruising along smoothly. Business was very good and I had enough money

Nick Carraway's Journal

to do what I wanted. The people I knew appeared to be generous to me, but I can now see they either wanted something, or disregarded money so much that they didn't care on what or whom they spent it.

Since coming back, I also had to learn the hardware business, essentially starting from the bottom. My mother was so delighted to have me home that it didn't matter what I had done. That I had survived the war and New York, and was home in one piece was enough for her.

My father knew that both those things were things I had to do, and he welcomed me back both as a son, and as someone he felt he could have absolute trust in as a business partner and successor. He patiently taught me the business, and I studied hard and learned it thoroughly because I knew I had nothing else to do, and nowhere else to go.

We spent a lot of time on the road driving to manufacturers, going to trade fairs, and visiting large customers. During those drives, or at quiet times in the office and at home, I told him the stories about Ridley, Pamela, the Drewsons, Tom, Daisy, the Wilsons and Gatsby. He listened and made no more comment than, "You were successful in the war; you were successful at the Probity Trust, and you'll do just fine here."

*

June 1928

It's not easy to think of your cousin as a

Undivulged Crimes

murderer. Technically, my silence in the matter makes me an accessory after the fact, but to what end would the prosecution of Daisy have accomplished anything, even justice? Wilson and his wife and Gatsby were dead. Tom went on believing whatever he wanted to believe, and Daisy had to live with the memory of running down Myrtle Wilson, and its terrible consequences.

How much Daisy was in control of her life after that evening, I never knew. That night, when I went to the Buchanans', I met Gatsby and had my last words with him. He really felt that Daisy needed him, but he couldn't bring himself to knock on the door, but then, neither could I. We could only speculate what was going on inside. Did Tom believe that Gatsby had been driving the car? Or did he know that Daisy was, and felt that he now had real power over her? I'm not sure anyone ever found out.

What I did realize, when I walked away from the house and drove, very carefully, back to my little cottage, was that Gatsby and Daisy were finally on equal terms. The gangster and his murdering moll. Gatsby and I knew it was indisputably murder, though neither of us said a syllable about it. Gatsby, of course, had been there, but my certainty was based on what I knew Daisy knew, and it produced a sickening dread in my bowels that I had not felt since I was in France.

The sad truth for Gatsby was that although he and Daisy now occupied the same criminal status, she still didn't want him.

Nick Carraway's Journal

She never did.
*

Tom and Daisy left the country so quickly that Daisy didn't have the chance to react to Gatsby's death. No one ever pursued her because no one ever knew of her guilt. There was no evidence. The only clue I had had come from Gatsby, and was now unverifiable.

I hung around New York for a while; I met Gatsby's father. Pamela and I spent some time together talking on my porch, no longer illuminated by the light reflected off Gatsby's white mansion, nor echoing to the intoxicating beat of the bands that had filled so many nights. We talked of various people, and about what we'd do next.

I knew that my time in the East was over. There no longer seemed to be any reason for me to stay there. Selling bonds suddenly seemed to be an empty and pointless activity. I worked until November, closed up my house, quit my job, said good-bye to the Drewsons and the regulars at the Yale Club, and moved back to Minneapolis. I was done seeking independence and adventure. If there were to be any more in my life, it would have to come to me.

February 1932

I continued to think of Tom, Daisy and Gatsby on and off, but the depression, the collapse of banks and the businesses and the grinding of the hardware business to nearly a full stop, had meant that self-indulgent reflections from nearly a decade earlier had to take a back

Undivulged Crimes

seat.

At the beginning of this month, the memories were brought to the surface again. I had a letter, out of the blue, from Faustina O'Brien. She had got my address from Pamela Drewson. It was just a short note with a cutting from the Paris Herald-Tribune. The note said, "Dear Nick, Will those times never stop haunting us? Love, F."

The cutting inside was short and announced the death of Thomas J. Buchanan, businessman, polo player and Yale man, from a self-inflicted gunshot wound. While details had not been confirmed, it was thought that the loss of his considerable fortune on Wall Street along with the collapse of businesses, banks and property values had been the main reason. Of Daisy and Pammy, there was no word.

Faustina had put a return address on her letter, so I contacted her to see if she knew any more. Daisy's family was all dead, and I didn't know Tom's people.

Faustina lived near Pittsburgh but had some family in the Midwest. When she replied, she suggested that she come to see me when she visited her brother and his family in a few weeks' time. I wasn't sure I wanted to see her. I had had mixed feelings about her in New York, and there were enough ghosts rattling around in my head without a real one showing up. I did remember that Faustina had been very pretty, and I was curious about how her life had turned out now that we were approaching forty. I wrote back and agreed to meet her at

Nick Carraway's Journal

the Curtis Hotel. Neutral ground.

I'd been in Minneapolis long enough to know a good number of people, so I wasn't surprised to see several of my acquaintance in the lobby also waiting to meet people, but more likely salesmen than former flappers. I was chatting to one of them when Faustina walked in.

Instantly ignoring Philbin, I stood up and watched her walk towards me. Though modestly dressed, she looked elegant with no detail of her hair, make-up or dress overlooked, or over-done. When she spotted me, she gave a big smile, reached out, grabbing my hand and kissed my cheeks. The European affectation seldom seen more than five miles inland on the East Coast was noticed by several people with a mixture of disdain and envy.

Philbin laughed loudly.

"Hell, Carraway! I thought you were meeting a hinge salesman."

Faustina and I left the hotel and headed to one of the better restaurants, chatting about nothing on the way. She slipped her arm through mine, as I remembered was her habit, and her voice had the same enchanting tone that I remembered.

Entering the restaurant, I noticed that several men looked up and watched her as we moved to a table. Even plainly dressed, she still had that effect on people.

"Those were curious times, weren't they?" she

Undivulged Crimes

said after we'd looked at the menus. "I thought life was going to be like that: troops of friends, parties, easy living." She gave an ironic laugh.

"You left right after the Gatsby business, didn't you? I stayed on until the crash. My boyfriend—I told everyone he was my fiancé—was one of the poor bastards who went out a window. We were all so young. I fled back to Pennsylvania, got an office job—which I am glad to still have—and go by my middle name. I'm just Mary O'Brien in a typing pool where the water's getting shallower every month."

I asked what she knew about the Gatsby story. As I suspected, she knew the public version and nothing about Daisy or Tom's involvement.

"Tom was a hulking brute, just like the book says," she said. "He'd go after just about any woman he saw. I had to push him off me at that first party I went to." She laughed. "Flattering, of course, but Tom had no taste, and there was no future there, and I was looking for a rich husband. By the time I left New York, no one was rich."

She asked me about business, family and anyone I knew from those faraway days. Then we began talking about Tom's suicide.

"How did you happen to get the clipping from Paris?" I asked.

"Diana sent it to me," she replied. "She was another one of us girls who had no place to get a good meal after Gatsby was dead. Several of

Nick Carraway's Journal

us shared a lot of bread and beans when it all collapsed. I thought you'd be interested and asked Pamela for your address."

"She was nice," I said. "Did she ever marry?"

"No, much to her parents' disappointment. Some people said she didn't like men, but that wasn't strictly true. She is just very self-contained. She liked you, and several other men."

"I liked her," I said. "A lot, but not enough."

"And me?" she asked, and I could sense the conversation moving quickly out of control. Faustina smiled. "You never trusted me, did you?"

I agreed.

"I thought you were just another silly flapper, but a pretty one who was nice to me."

She looked at me with her lively blue eyes and said, "Poor Nick. You were the wise one who saw it all heading for disaster and couldn't do anything about it. After the war, it must have been hard to see the self-destruction at home. You never preached, but you knew, and people knew you knew, but didn't want to know."

"I didn't disapprove," I said. "I never judged anyone--"

"But a lot of people could see what you thought."

"Oh, I don't think so."

Undivulged Crimes

"Pamela did. Daisy did. I did," she said. "And I still do."

❦

This entry was one of the most shocking of Dad's journal. [Daisy says it was *the* most shocking.] We knew Mother as Mary O'Brien, and Dad always called her Mary, at least around us. That our mother from the Pittsburgh typing pool had been one of Gatsby's hangers-on, and one whom Dad had regarded with scorn, took us some getting used to.

❦

Faustina didn't know where Daisy was but thought Pammy, who would now have been about twelve, was at a boarding school in Switzerland, but couldn't remember who had told her. I reckoned that only Yale could help me trace Tom's family and that would help me find Daisy. I felt awkward about doing it, but Daisy and Pammy were relatives and I owed it to them.

Faustina's words in the restaurant had surprised me. That she paid any notice of anything I said or did was a whole new thought.

"Of course, Nick!" she exclaimed. "You were our conscience. I could measure my behavior by the way you looked at me. It was the fact you never said anything disapproving that made the impression: you only looked sad."

I hardly knew how to reply to that, and so said nothing.

Nick Carraway's Journal

"You see!" she said with her rich laugh. "You're doing it now! I've actually missed that look. I'm afraid it didn't make me act much better, but it was somehow reassuring to have my personal Cassandra who didn't need to speak." She paused and looked at my face, then down at her hands which were toying with a coffee spoon.

"I'm quite different now," she said softly. "I live at home; I work hard; I sew and mend my clothes; cook supper for my parents and spend very little on myself. We weren't rich like Tom and Daisy, but we're just about broke."

She looked up tentatively and gave a slight smile.

"The Drewson's are still all right. They were very careful with their money. Generous, but not careless. Pamela's job ended when all her customers lost their money and jobs. She's become reclusive. What she needs is a nice widowed European count or something. Someone who is undemanding and can see her for her qualities and not her money. That's what I think she needs."

"And what do you need?" I ventured.

"The same thing as you."

*

November 1932

Happy Days Are Here Again? We shall see. Things could be much worse, but when Governor

Undivulged Crimes

Roosevelt becomes president things might change, but not quickly. I think.

My efforts to trace Daisy went more slowly than I'd hoped. Tom's family didn't reply to my letter, but a few weeks ago I had a letter from a man I'd never heard of called Charles Sandler. He wrote from Philadelphia and explained that he was married to Tom's sister. I didn't know Tom had a sister. (Further proof that he talked only of himself). Tom's parents didn't want to discuss anything to do with him, but they maintained the fiction that he was living in Europe and would probably stay there. Susan, the sister, didn't want to talk about Tom either because she believed that Daisy had refused to give Tom any of her money once his had run out. Susan maintained, her husband wrote, that Daisy had become more irrational and irresponsible both towards herself and Pammy. Pammy was in a Swiss boarding school, and Daisy was now a few miles down the lake in a private sanatorium where she had surrendered herself and her reason.

Sandler wrote without comment in a language that suggested he was a lawyer: neutral and informative, but it was a language that also shut the door on further query or correspondence. I have no doubt that he told me everything he knew, but it left me without an idea of how to contact Pammy.

I wrote to every school I could find the name and address for around Lake Geneva. One day, one wrote back saying that Pamela Buchanan had been at the school for several years and had remained after her father's death, but after

Nick Carraway's Journal

her mother's committal, Pamela had been released into the care of Mme. Cardillac as per the terms set out by the family's solicitors.

I wrote again for more information and the name of the solicitors and some indication of who Mme. Cardillac was. I did not hear from them again.

I didn't see what else I could do. I wrote several insistent letters to the Buchanans and Charles Sandler, reminding them I was family. I also had a letter published in the Yale Alumni Magazine that included all the relevant names, dates and other details. Several people wrote saying that they had known Tom, but none had any knowledge of him after he left America.

I confess that at this time, I was also distracted by a romantic involvement that was as unexpected as it was compelling. Based on our brief meeting, I had kept in touch with Faustina. She made more frequent trips to see her brother's family, and eventually managed to secure a job in Minneapolis, in another typing pool at a local insurance company. It allowed us to have time together that wasn't rushed, or colored by absence. Both bruised in circumstances the other understood perfectly well, we slowly revealed our post-twenties selves and found an understanding that continued to deepen.

October 1978

There were several pages after this one, but they were cloyingly sentimental and more

Undivulged Crimes

suited to a high school sophomore than a man in his thirties. The salient facts are that Faustina and I were married in the optimistic gloom of 1933 and we began making a home and tried to keep what we could of the business going.

Every so often there would be a story in the newspaper or the Saturday Evening Post that referred to Gatsby and the triple deaths. One or two even suggested that things were not as they had been reported, but offered neither theories nor evidence. However, these allowed Faustina and me to reflect again on that summer of 1925.

We read of others from that time dying: Meyer Wolfsheim (of a heart attack at a racetrack); the Drewsons (about a month apart, both aged over ninety); Bunsen (during the Second World War); and one day, Daisy Buchanan's death was reported. It was a four-inch article, mostly about how the death of her husband a decade before had caused her mental breakdown. She died of undisclosed causes in the sanatorium where she had been for twenty years. There was no mention of a daughter.

Yet again, I wrote a number of letters to see if I could pick up a lead, but nothing materialized.

By chance, in late 1958, I saw a fuzzy photo in a New York newspaper on a society page with the engagement announcement of a Pamela Cardillac, of Philadelphia, to a New York broker.

Nick Carraway's Journal

Even if this were Pammy, there was no point in contacting her now. She would be well looked after, as I suspected she had always been. I could offer nothing but unpleasant memories.

ଛ

It surprised us that Dad accepted that Daisy had killed Myrtle Wilson. He had, of course, seen her take the wheel, and Gatsby was desperate to protect her, which he ultimately did, though she never escaped the horrors.

I guess they *were* careless people from a careless age; an age framed by two world wars and a depression. Enough to make memories and the common perception of the period suspect. Yet, there are the films, the photographs, the newspapers and the music that make reconstruction of that past almost possible.

Hardest to accept is the idea of Mother as a flapper of whom Father disapproved. We never thought she was much different than anyone else's mother. Hard working; strict, but fair; frugal and resourceful; it was hard to imagine her spending lots of money on party dresses, feathered headbands, long beads, drinking bootleg gin and dancing with abandon at scandalous all-night parties.

In theory, we know our parents have pasts, and in reality, they are pasts similar to our own lives, give or take a world war, a great depression or a murder. Yet, even with Dad's comments and insights, Jay Gatsby remains elusive and evermore enigmatic.

Undivulged Crimes

The Gemini Experiment

Undivulged Crimes

The Gemini Experiment

Now that there are no longer any "O" level examinations and I am secure in my retirement, there are a few things I want to set down. Not a confession, but an admission. I regret nothing and my secret has given me pleasure for thirty-two years.

I always thought "O" level exams were nonsense. Anyone with half a brain could see whether a pupil knew his stuff. The machinery of the great university examining boards was ludicrous, expensive and wide-open to corruption. How many publishers bribed examiners to list their editions as set texts?

Then there was the bluff about objectivity: elaborate charades with centre numbers and unknown examiners, not to mention a total lack of accountability. It was paradise for those in charge, and hell for those at the receiving end. I once saw an examiner's report on a pupil claiming that he had made a particular mess of question No. 37. Appalled by the lad's stupidity, I took a copy of the report and the exam paper to the boy and demanded to know how he could have bungled that problem.

"I couldn't have bungled it, sir," the lad answered, "I did the other option. I never did No. 37 at all."

I wrote this up for the board, and had the headmaster

send it in, demanding a full explanation. Needless to say, we never had any reply at all, but all our candidates passed for the next two years.

As soon as I realised the complete immunity that examiners enjoyed, I applied for a position. Marking maths papers doesn't take much intelligence and not a lot of time.

It was a quick and easy way to finance a colour television, or a week or two in Majorca.

When I got my first batch of scripts in June, all I could see was the pound signs and the hot Mediterranean sun. After the first hundred scripts, my eyes began to rebel against the tangle of scrawl.

As I said, the marking itself was a doddle, but I had to do something to relieve the tedium. It couldn't be too obvious because the work was double-checked. It would be carefully checked, too, since I was brand new. Eventually, I would work my way to the top where I would do the checking, and I wanted a scheme which would work even then.

Like all brilliant solutions, I found it by accident. I was adding up the marks of a particularly good pupil and checked the name and thought I had already marked that paper once. Looking back, I found that there were two girls of the same surname in the group.

A possibility began to form in my mind. Checking

The Gemini Experiment

the cover sheets, I determined that the girls shared the same birthday. It was unlikely that they were anything but twins.

I compared the papers: one, Jane, showed flair, accuracy and real ability. She had a mark of 78, which would probably qualify her for an "A". The other, Joyce, was clearly an artist. While creative, her approaches were intuitive and not mathematically logical. Her mark was 39, a certain fail.

On my master marking sheet, I simply switched them. Joyce would get an "A" while her clever sister would fail.

The chances of this "error" being caught was minimal: the examiner would study the test papers, not the result sheet. The marks on the papers would be correct, a slip of the pen would account for the error on the marking sheet. I laughed out loud at the scheme. It was simple and diabolical. I could amuse myself and thumb my nose at the stupid system simultaneously.

That evening on the way home, I bought a little blue bound notebook. On the first page I wrote "The Gemini Experiment, 1954 – ". On the second page, I wrote, "June 1954, Leyton Grammar School, Jane Lewis 39; Joyce Lewis 78."

I looked through the remainder of my papers, but there were no other twins. I drew a line under the first entry.

Undivulged Crimes

As August approached, I spent many quiet moments wondering what the scene would be like at the Lewis house when the marks arrived. Joyce would clearly be elated, but what of Jane?

Crushed? Heart-broken? Relieved? Was she planning to do maths at "A" level? Forget that. Would she now fall short of her five "O" level passes required for admission to the sixth form? Pity. Or would she be enormously relieved since all she wanted was to be a hair-dresser, and marry the bloke at the petrol station?

With a stroke of the pen I might have dashed her hopes, or made her dreams come true.

There was only a slight chance that the school would question the result. In three decades, I never ceased to be appalled by the unquestioning attitude schools had towards examination boards.

There was still the chance that Jane would re-take the exam the following November. It was unlikely that I would be sent the script to mark, but it was possible.

In the event, there was no trouble.

When the November papers arrived, I read the names and was delighted to find two sets of twins, which was unusual since far fewer pupils took exams in November.

One pair was from a grammar school and the

The Gemini Experiment

other from a posh girls' school in the Midlands, if such a thing is possible.

Doreen and Tracey Baxter were both hopeless at maths and I had to fail both of them. No way round that, more's the pity; but, Barbara and Margaret Hammel were both fairly good. Barbara scored 70 and Margaret scored 62. Depending how the allocation fell, both marks could conceivably be "B" grades. With little hope of any success with these two, I switched their marks.

In early April, I went to an examiners' meeting and took the opportunity to consult the records of the re-takes. I found that no one from Leyton had re-taken maths that year. Jane could have gone to a crammer or entered through night school, but that was a fairly remote chance, especially for someone from Leyton.

Speculating on Joyce and Jane amused me, but reading on through the lists, I found I had an unexpected bonus. The division between grade "B" and grade "C" fell at 65 marks. That meant that Margaret Hammel would have received a "B" and her sister, Barbara, a "C".

What fun this was!

Ambitions thwarted, futures changed. Pupils encouraged to pursue the wrong field of study and others kept from careers where they might have shown real ability.

I could play God from a bed-sit in Ealing.

ଔ

Over the years, the game became easier to play, not

more difficult. The pages of my blue notebook began to fill with names. Many twins scored comparably and there was nothing I could do with them. I never gratuitously reduced or enhanced anyone's marks in all my time as an examiner. However, there were enough variations to keep things interesting.

There was a danger of being discovered, but this was part of the excitement. Exam results seldom turn out the way one expects. This stems from the preposterous system, rather than from the actual performance of any individual candidate.

Several weeks before the exam was set, the chief examiners and other members of the bureaucracy would get together to determine what percentage of those taking exams would pass. Usually about fifty-five per cent would pass, but sometimes it would be as much as fifty-eight per cent or as little as fifty. What the rules governing these figures were, I never in all my time with the board ever determined. Anyway, of the number that would pass, the top ten per cent would get "A"s, the next fifteen per cent, "B"s; the next thirty per cent, "C"s.

Over time, there have been variations, but the point is, whatever messing about with the marks I did, was nothing compared to what the pros did. Sometimes their grade bands would be so stretched as to make a nonsense of my efforts. Sometimes

The Gemini Experiment

bands would be so narrow that my "adjustments" would become frighteningly obvious. One year, there was a public outcry because some examiner betrayed his trust and revealed that the "C" band was only three marks wide. This meant that a pupil with a mark of 63 was awarded a "B" while one with a 60 would receive a "D" and consequently fail.

The injustice of it all.

༂

There was a certain scientific value to what I was doing. Male twins achieved more consistently similar marks than did female twins. Of mixed twins, girls scored markedly better than their brothers – except on the papers I marked. After ten years, I abandoned swopping the marks of male twins altogether. Only female and mixed twins were included in this phase of the experiment.

I followed the progress of my twins carefully.

I found those who had retaken the exams and recorded their retake marks in my notes. Occasionally, I would find that I had to mark the retake of a girl I had made a victim. In that case, I had to mark honestly and fairly. Once in a while, to my joy, they would do as badly as their sister had done in the original exam. I put this down to the then popular "self-fulfilling prophecy" phenomenon. Clearly, the experience of apparent failure in the first round had brought about the actual failure in the second.

Undivulged Crimes

My experiment, you see, was not without psychological and sociological interest and merit.

During the summer of 1964, I had an unexpected bonus: Carol, Lucy and Jennifer – the Wilson triplets.

I had never marked the papers of a set of triplets before and it presented me with an entirely new set of problems: since they weren't twins, should I exclude them from my enterprise? To be scrupulously bound by the rule – my own rule – only to switch the marks of twins seemed Pecksniffian: but to include them led to further decisions: should I just switch the top one with the bottom one, leaving the middle one with her earned mark? Or should I rotate the grades all around?

The first problem I resolved by deciding to include the Wilson triplets in my experiment. As to the second question, I decided to mark their papers first, then decide. If their scores were close, there would be no point in doing anything.

Both Lucy and Carol had marks of 79. However, as I began Jennifer's paper I realised that this girl was not the dedicated mathematician that her sisters were. There were doodles in the margins and her initials in pencilled hearts together with some boy's. Jennifer's mind was somewhere else. She would pass, but only just.

There was danger in this case. If Carol and Lucy

The Gemini Experiment

were known to be good, and Jennifer known to be scatty, then a mix-up would look obvious.

Reluctantly, I decided that a straight swap was impossible. On the mark sheets next to Carol and Lucy, I wrote "56"; next to Jennifer, I put "79". The marks on the papers, I left unaltered, as always.

Rather Draconian, I know. But with Lucy and Carol performing comparably, Jennifer's mark would look like a typical "O" level fluke. Chances of any of the marks being questioned were reduced to the minimum.

Mathematicians love knotty problems, and I was pleased with this solution.

෨

Computers were the next innovation of the examination boards and they scared me. Surely, they would tumble to what I was doing. I had another twelve years before retirement and was moving up the ranks of the examination structure. I was now in a position to alter the marks of twins from five dozen schools.

The experiment was now in its twentieth year and I had never been caught. The triplets had accepted their fate and Carol and Lucy did not re-take their exams. It was that damn computer which caused me the most anxiety. I eagerly read all the bumpf; I went to the examiners' seminar explaining how it worked, and combed the *Times Ed.* to learn more about it.

I needn't have worried.

Undivulged Crimes

In the first year, that machine juggled more marks than I could have in a millennium. Everything had to be re-done by hand, just as it always had been, and two more pairs of twins had their marks switched.

My notebook was two thirds full. Seventy-six sets of twins had taken part in the Gemini Experiment. I hoped to reach a hundred-twenty-five before retirement. It was possible, for now, as a deputy chief examiner, I had virtually unlimited access to the lists.

As the years passed, I became increasingly curious about the effect of the switched marks. How had it altered lives, if it had at all? Had their happiness been markedly affected? Did any of it matter?

It seemed a good project for my retirement: somehow, I would trace the twins and find out what they were doing. The idea had appeal and would help to fill the hours once occupied with marking.

That pleasure was still several years off.

Governments came and went and with them radical changes in education. Yet, the "O" levels remained, and so did I.

At one point it looked like the experiment was done for. I was offered the job of Chief Examiner. While that would give me enviable control of the syllabus and the exam itself, but it would remove me from any actual marking, and be the end of the Gemini Experiment.

The Gemini Experiment

Reluctantly, I declined the offer, but the board was pleased that I would remain as deputy.

༄

Every year, in August, there is at least one tragic story in the newspapers. It appears with such regularity that one suspects that it is a formula story with blanks for the details. It is the article about some teenager who has killed himself (or, herself) in despair over examination results.

All examiners read these articles carefully to see, if by chance, it is someone whose paper they have marked. Each year, one examiner has to come to terms with the fact that his marking stimulated the wasteful and desperate action.

It is not the examiner's fault that pupils do badly on their exams, but the connection between the examiner and the pupil in these cases is so close that a degree of responsibility, if not culpability, is inevitable.

I have watched these articles especially carefully.

It was in the very August after my retirement that Allison Warner, one of the last twins in the experiment, died of an over-dose of Valium.

Her death was a lesson to me which was long overdue. There was no way round my direct responsibility.

Allison had a conditional acceptance to a well-known Public School that admitted girls to its Sixth Form. She needed five good "O" levels, including "B"s in English and

Undivulged Crimes

maths. I had given Allison her sister's 48 and Gretchen, Allison's 73.

There was no way I could expunge my guilt, though I did find it necessary to cover my tracks. I still had access to the files and I altered the marks on the examiner's sheet to show the correct marks. If discovered, it would now look like a clerical error at worst or a computer error at best.

I very nearly burned my notebook.

However, a plan came to me which would marginally assuage my conscience while at the same time inflict a final tweak on the despicable examination board.

I had begun to trace the twins. It wasn't too difficult as few of them had moved far from home. Since many were female, it did mean that many surnames were different, which slowed things down. I had plenty of time, and reading documents and sifting through newspapers, telephone directories and census reports was not strenuous work. When all else failed, I'd try calling relatives on the telephone to learn current addresses. Telling people that I was from the Premium Bond office assured co-operation.

Of the hundred and thirty-two sets of twins (yes, I made my goal with a few to spare), all but five were still alive. I had recent addresses for all but a dozen pairs.

The Gemini Experiment

With foresight, I had stolen a ream of Examination Board stationery, and with the aid of my home computer, I composed the following form letter.

CENTRAL LONDON EXAMINATION BOARD
ACADEMIC HOUSE TOWER HILL ROAD SE 5 7BQ

```
Dear _____,

For the past thirty years, the Central
London Examination Board has been run-
ning a research project known as "The
Gemini Experiment".

The Gemini Experiment has involved 132
sets of twins. In your "O" level year,
certain exam grades were deliberately
swapped with your twin brother/sister.
In your case, it was the . . . . . . .
mark which was switched.

We are now processing follow-up material
and would be interested to learn if the
course of your career was significantly
influenced by this change.

Please notify the board of any comments
you have, stating whether or not you re-
sat the examination and the result of
that re-take.

Please reply to the Director of the
```

Undivulged Crimes

```
Central London Examination Board at the
above address.
Yours sincerely,
```

I merged in the names of the ex-pupils and handwrote "mathematics". I felt it was a nice touch to imply that changes had been made in other subjects as well. The newspapers will have a field day with the story. The director of the board will, no doubt resign. There will probably even be questions raised in the House.

It's good to have a little excitement in one's retirement. I wish I could read some of the twins' replies, but I shall have to content myself with following the stories in the papers.

I'm lucky that so many English newspapers are available in Majorca.

The Benefactor

The Benefactor

Undivulged Crimes

The Benefactor

Lucinda Lord paid no more attention to news of the crash than any other of the dozen disasters which assaulted her that week via the media. In this instance, it was the crash of an aircraft in the Mediterranean. Some terrorist group was alleged to have blown it up in mid-air, and sent two hundred people to premature deaths.

Lucinda was not insensitive; she felt the vague sort of pity for the friends and families of the victims, and even a little sorrow for the victims themselves. After all, it couldn't have been the holiday they expected.

Having mourned the requisite thirty seconds and indulged in two additional minutes' discussion of the gory details on the underground on her way to work, Lucinda let other bad news replace it in the forefront of her mind.

By the time a pin-striped chap appeared on her doorstep six weeks later, she had long forgotten it completely.

"Miss Lord?"

"Yes."

"Miss Lucinda Lord?"

"Yes.

"May I ask you a rather odd question?"

She eyed him carefully, but he did not seem about to pull a cleaver from under his waistcoat.

Undivulged Crimes

"All right."

"Did you have a dog named Bertram when you were young?"

At twenty-four, she did not exactly like the way he had phrased it, but answered.

"Yes, but – "

"Miss Lord," he said with somewhat embarrassed officiousness, "this is not the sort of conversation which should be conducted on the front steps. May I come in?"

"Could you please tell me who you are?" she asked, meeting officiousness with officiousness – and a hint of mockery.

"I am sorry. I'm rather off form on this one. Frankly, I've been worried about asking you about that stupid dog all day. It's not at all the sort of thing I'm used to."

"Bertram was not a stupid dog! In fact, he was quite clever and rather sweet," she said with indignation and firmly began to close the door.

"My name is Nigel Woodstock. I represent the Edgeware Life Assurance – please, Miss Lord, don't shut the door until you hear the rest of the sentence – Company, plc, and I promise that I am not selling insurance."

Here he had had to pause for breath, but he used the time to look appealingly at Miss Lord, which he found not at all difficult.

"No sales?"

"I promise."

The Benefactor

She nodded sceptically and led him into the sitting room. He wasn't bad, for an insurance type. Rather distinguished for a youngish man, and it was clear that he was less than confident about what ever business brought him to her flat.

Ten minutes, she thought, glancing at her Gucci watch (green today), resolving to allow herself the full ninety minutes expected of her to get ready for her dinner engagement.

Inside, Nigel Woodstock set his briefcase on his knees.

"You are Lucinda Lord, and you did have a dog called Bertram?"

"Yes, but I fail to see – "

"Then let me first offer my sympathy in your bereavement. I know that nothing can compensate for your loss, but perhaps what I have to say will help you more quickly to recover."

Nigel Woodstock knew that with certain classes one must be certain not to carelessly split infinitives.

"Mr Woodstock, I have no idea what you are talking about!" answered Lucinda of the class allowed to dangle prepositions.

"I have here an insurance policy – "

She stood up abruptly.

"That's it! Out! You insurance types are all the same!"

Undivulged Crimes

"Miss Lord, I told you; I am not trying to sell you anything. You are the beneficiary of a considerable policy."

"Oh dear!" she exclaimed, sitting down again. "I suppose that means someone has died."

"You mean you don't know?"

"Not a relative, I hope?"

"Mr Carroll was not a relative, I believe?"

"Who?"

"Harold T. Carroll, Jr."

"Sounds American," she mused under her breath.

"Indeed, he was. But you don't know him?"

"I don't think so."

It was getting late and it looked as though this might take some time. Even Nigel Woodstock was fast losing interest in this case. As it was, the company wouldn't mind forgetting about it either.

"Look, I have a policy here taken out by Mr Carroll which names you," he said, checking his papers, "Miss Lucinda Lord, of the Sloane Square area of London, England, who in her childhood was possessed of a dog called Bertram."

"I suppose that's me," Lucinda said, abandoning grammar altogether.

"As far as the Edgeware Life Assurance Company – "

"– plc – "

"Thank you – is concerned, it's you," he said. "Are you sure you don't know him?"

The Benefactor

"What does he look like?"

"We have no idea. He bought his policy at one of those little machines at Heathrow."

"And he's dead?"

"Oh, yes. He was on that plane which was blown up a few weeks ago. You are to receive the total sum assured."

"A few extra quid is always welcome. Porcelain mending doesn't pay as well as one might think, and Daddy has been getting ratty about the overdrafts."

"Madam," Woodstock said in his most serious tones, modelled on those he fancied would follow the ringing of the Lutine bell at Lloyds, "five hundred thousand pounds is hardly to be classed as a 'few quid.'"

"No," Lucinda considered, "it certainly is not. But who was Harold T. Carroll?"

"Junior."

"Junior. Thank you."

"Miss Lord, I don't know who he was, though I dare say head office does. It has been determined that you are entitled to the money. If you wish to pursue that matter, that is up to you. I don't."

He closed his case and stood up.

"The Edgeware Life Assurance Company plc is not a missing persons bureau nor a detective agency. Frankly, we do not like giving money away – especially since it appears that this policy was the product of mere whimsy which turned out to be more lucky for you than for Mr Carroll."

"Woodstock," she said coldly, "you have no cause to be short with me, but since you have, may I recommend a good nerve specialist in Harley Street – "

"Forgive me, Miss Lord. From beginning to end this particular case has been a nightmare. Not just the money, but the dealings with the police."

"Police?"

"Edgeware Life Assurance Company plc took considerable pains to run interference on your behalf."

"But why?"

"Well, frankly, you had to be investigated."

"Mr Woodstock, you go too far!"

"No, indeed, dear lady. When an airplane blows up, the authorities always look to see who benefits. Apart from the news media, you Miss Lord, have benefited more than anyone else from the mishap."

"Oh, dear."

"Oh, dear, indeed, Miss Lord."

She thought a moment.

"May I infer from the payment that I am judged to be innocent."

"*Uninvolved*," Nigel Woodstock corrected.

"As you say, Mr Woodstock."

"Well, enjoy your money, Miss Lord," Woodstock said, handing over the cheque, "and be careful."

The Benefactor

"Thank you, Nigel."

"Any time, Lucinda."

༄

Lucinda was a little annoyed with Nigel for becoming ruffled by her questions. It wasn't her fault that she hadn't the slightest notion of what he was talking about. Still, she thought, they parted well.

He was nice, but an insurance man. Never mind, she could change that if she had to. If she wanted to.

In spite of the fact that Lucinda had little to do to ready herself for the dinner party, it fully took the allocated ninety minutes. She laid out her clothes, bathed, did her hair, and put on her make-up. That took forty-five minutes. She made a gin and tonic (three minutes); then attempted to fill her evening bag with her "survival kit" (three minutes: it was a very small bag); finding the contents took forty-five minutes. When she found her watch (now black, for mourning) she was three minutes behind. She rushed through the flat, drank her (now iceless) G & T (fifteen seconds), grabbed the insurance cheque, an envelope, her keys, and ran out the door towards the Sloane Square underground station.

On the tube, she looked for her pen, but couldn't find it. She addressed the envelope to Hoares, St James, with eyebrow pencil, stuck on every 2p stamp left in her very old purse and endorsed the cheque. ("Geoff - a bit of good

Undivulged Crimes

luck (and bad, I'll explain later) please credit to my current a/c, Lucinda Wyndham Lord").

She posted the letter outside Hampstead tube station and continued her way to Samantha's.

With any luck, she thought, she'd forget about the money and enjoy herself.

Samantha was a school friend who now worked at a fashionable antique shop with the too trendy name, "ANTIQUE."

Samantha's parties were usually good: not too rowdy; not too dull; not too crowded, and large enough that if one wanted, one didn't have to talk to a soul all night. Her flat was at the top of the small sixties shopping precinct, and had large windows opening on to a very small balcony which, eventually, overlooked the Heath, or very nearly.

Samantha's lack of furniture was notorious in her crowd. She slept on a mattress, and apart from a stereo centre and a television, she had no furniture at all.

"I'm twenty-five and I have moved eleven times since I left school. I got sick of it, and gave away all my furniture."

This view found much sympathy except when people came to visit and had to sit on the floor, or eat on it, or sleep on it. She had many complaints from her employer who was besieged by clients whom she had entertained.

The Benefactor

"If I am to entertain clients," Samantha had charmingly argued, "I should be given a budget for it; then I could take them out to eat. Unless, of course, you would like to furnish my flat with things from the shop, in which case it would be another showroom for you. However, I would have to charge you for storage...."

Her offer was declined, but clients were still entertained there and complained later. The empty flat did have the advantage of being spacious for parties and since there were no chairs, no one was left without one.

Samantha herself was one of Lucinda's oldest friends. They had been through all the usual trials at school together, and had half-heartedly done the deb scene as well. Apart from a liking of antiques, they had little in common except their past, but that was enough to keep them reasonably close. Their temperaments were similar, neither one given to histrionics; they both had good senses of humour and, perhaps most importantly, they had different tastes in men.

Lucinda entered the flat clutching a cheap bottle of Spanish plonk, and looked around to see if there was anyone she knew there (more accurately, she looked to see if there was anyone there whom she did not know).

As she made her way to the kitchen in search of a corkscrew, she spoke to a number of people briefly, but when she came to Samantha, she grabbed her firmly by the arm and dragged her away from some army smarmy and led her into the kitchen.

"That might have cost me a regimental ball," Samantha snapped.

"Thank me later," Lucinda said, as she rooted through the collection of bottles on the counter for the corkscrew. Finding it, she opened the bottle and poured the rough red into two paper cups.

"Here," she said, giving one to Samantha. "I'll be with you in a moment."

She drank half of it, coughed and put the cup down.

"God, that's awful."

"Dreadful," Samantha agreed, gasping for breath. "Now, what's so urgent?"

"Were you at that party where there was some middle-aged Yank who worked for an oil company?"

"When was this? There are so many."

"About two months ago, I think."

"Whose party was it?"

"That's the trouble. I wish I could remember. Some people from the Chinese embassy were there and got into a row with Justin Southworth. I think Lucia was there with Caroline and I think you were there for a while, too."

"For a while?"

"I think you had a better party to go to that night, but wanted to put in an appearance and test your make-up."

The Benefactor

"Oh, that one!" she exclaimed. "That was at Miranda's."

Samantha leaned over to consult a calendar on the wall.

"Yes, that was February fifth. Are you trying to trace this Yank?"

"Yes."

"You're not old enough to be that desperate. He was dreadfully dull."

"Was he a friend of Miranda?" Lucinda asked.

"Who knows? She gets such a strange crowd. She should be here tonight."

"I've got to talk to her."

Lucinda started from the kitchen, but Samantha stopped her.

"Hey, vague-ape! What's this all about? You can't go secretive on me now."

"Sam, it's dreadful. Well, it's good but it's ghastly."

"Oh, well, that explains it."

"It's serious."

"You and a colonial serious?"

"No, stupid," Lucinda shrugged her shoulders in despair. "Okay, I'll tell you, but it's super-secret. Not a word. Blood oath."

"Promise."

The reversion to the school girl code signalled something serious, indeed, and as much as Samantha's sophistication would want her to tell it all to the first person she saw, she would not.

"Come!" Lucinda dragged Samantha though the crowd again and led her into the bathroom and locked the door.

"What are you doing?" Samantha demanded. "We're not in the Lower Fourth anymore!"

"Shut up! I told you this is totally confidential. I shouldn't tell anyone, but I have to," Lucinda said. "That Yank was killed in that aeroplane explosion, the one over the Mediterranean."

Samantha covered her mouth in horror.

"Oh, Cindy, I had no idea – I'm sorry – "

"It's not like that. I only saw him at the party and that was for all of half an hour."

"Then what's the problem?"

Lucinda told her.

"Half a million pounds? Oh, my dear, the taxes will ruin you."

"I can afford that now. There'll still be plenty left," Lucinda said. "But, what I want to know is who this Harold T. Carroll, Jr was, and why he decided to leave me all that money."

"That's why you wanted to know whose friend he was!"

"You're slow, Sam, but you get it in the end," Lucinda said. "But you mustn't tell anyone about the money."

The Benefactor

"Why ever not? It's super news!"

"Do you think I want everyone to know I'm loaded? I don't want to turn into a loan agency, or have every poverty-stricken peer of the realm chasing me?"

"I hadn't thought about that."

"No, I can see you hadn't."

"You can quit your job now and get out of that grotty flat," Samantha said enthusiastically.

"What's wrong with my flat? I like it. And, as for work, how am I supposed to spend my time? Sitting on philanthropic committees? No, I think I'll go on pretty much as usual until something better comes along. I never intended to spend my whole life mending pottery."

Someone knocked on the bathroom door.

"Just a minute, cretin!" shouted Samantha. "We're not finished in here yet!"

"And you think you're going to get the information out of Miranda?" Samantha asked.

"Carroll might have been a good friend of hers."

"A Yank? Is it likely?"

"It's possible, though not very."

"There is one other thing," Lucinda began cautiously.

"Well?"

"I've been investigated. They wanted to be certain that I wasn't part of the gang."

"But you've always been part of the gang," Samantha protested.

Undivulged Crimes

"No, clot, the terrorist gang!"

"Oh. Scary."

"Indeed."

"I might be followed. They might find out who I am. I could end up like one of those dreadful German women, you know, Baader-Meinhof."

"I've never known a terrorist before," Samantha said.

The knocking at the door became more urgent.

"Shut up!" Samantha shouted through the door. "I hope you won't let this interfere with our trip."

"No, of course not."

The impatient knocking was now a desperate banging.

"I guess we have to go," Lucinda said.

"I resent being kicked out of my own loo!" Samantha said opening the door. "Some people are so inconsiderate."

ಌ

Miranda did not show up at the party so Lucinda had to seek her out. It was after midnight when Lucinda arrived at Miranda's flat off Beauchamp Place. She had to lean on the bell for five minutes before the lock buzzed to let her in. Miranda was waiting on the top floor landing by the time Lucinda had climbed the five flights. She was dressed only in a lacy full-length red satin nightgown, but still completely made-up.

"Do you always let people in after midnight without finding out who they are first?"

The Benefactor

"Oh, hello, Cindy, what brings you here?"

"Isn't it dangerous?" she insisted, being a very cautious girl.

"Safer than walking the streets after midnight. Also, safer than waking people up at all hours, besides, by the time someone made it to the top floor, they're usually too tired to try anything."

"That sounds like bitter experience."

Miranda yawned.

"Come in before the neighbours start complaining. I'm in enough trouble with them already because of that last party."

Lucinda sensed that she shouldn't go into the apartment, but the day's events had completely re-ordered her sense of priorities and, it seemed, proprieties. Confidently, she strode into the flat.

Miranda's flat was opulent. On the top floor of the luxurious, but staid, Victorian "Consort Mansions," it was filled with mediaeval and Louis quatorze furniture. Even now, candles shone in mirrored and gilt sconces, and in large candlesticks which at one time had stood in private chapels. Lucinda felt there was something vaguely sacrilegious about their presence in Miranda's flat. Large pieces of furniture and wooden gothic arches loomed in the shadows.

Undivulged Crimes

"Actually, it's about that party that I came tonight," Lucinda said in her most perfect accent and formal tones. She did not want to lose the upper hand in this exchange.

Too often had her good nature been imposed upon by Miranda, whose very apartment was testimony to the fact that she was used to getting her own way.

"At your party, I met an American gentleman," Lucinda began, seating herself elegantly in the corner of a brocaded sofa, which was so precious a thing to Miranda that she frequently made guests bathe before allowing them to sit on it. "Since then, he has rather forced his attentions on me."

"You should be able to handle that sort of thing by now, old thing," Miranda answered abstractedly, glancing toward her bedroom.

"He told me so little about himself," Lucinda said.

"That's positively un-American," Miranda replied, not trying to hide her boredom.

"Have you got something to drink?" Lucinda asked, enjoying Miranda's growing discomfort and growing in the realisation that she had five hundred thousand reasons not to be to be intimidated – more by now, at today's interest rates.

"I don't think so," Miranda answered.

"Surely you have some tonic water."

"Very well. Wait here, I'll get it."

The Benefactor

Miranda went to the kitchen. In the silence of her absence, Lucinda heard someone padding about the bedroom.

Lucinda was not one to judge the affairs of others, but she did want to ascertain if there were someone else in the flat, hence her sudden thirst. Now that she knew, she also knew that she could not now tell Miranda the whole story, even had she been tempted.

She passed the rest of the time waiting for Miranda wondering whether or not to spill some of the tonic on the sofa. She hadn't yet decided when Miranda returned.

"No lime? Never mind."

Miranda sat in a hooded armchair and lit a Black Russian which she exhaled with some vehemence through her nostrils. Lucinda responded by taking her time lighting one of her Fribourg & Treyers.

"What can you tell me about Harry?" Lucinda asked.

Miranda watched the smoke rise for about half a minute before answering.

"What has he told you?"

"That he's in oil."

"And?"

"He's not poor."

"And?"

"That he likes me."

"Lord, couldn't you have rung me about this in the morning?"

Undivulged Crimes

"No."

Miranda considered this.

"Was he a friend of Lucia's?"

"That cow? What would she be doing knowing Harry?"

"Samantha said – "

"Samantha would," Miranda said impatiently. "You've known that girl for years; you must know that she never gets a story right. I met Harry at the Lansdowne a few months ago. He was working with Justin on some project or other. I invited him along to the party. I expect he's rich. Oil men tend to be. He left shortly after the fight. That's all I know."

Miranda stood up, moved to the door and opened it. Lucinda didn't flinch.

"Fight?" she asked, puzzled.

"*The* fight – perhaps you had gone by then, I wasn't paying attention to you."

"The fight? The one with the Chinese?"

"What Chinese? Was that Samantha again?" Miranda asked.

Lucinda nodded.

Miranda responded with one of her most bored expressions and blew a cloud of smoke toward the chandelier.

"Harry was telling some Arabs about the new plan to develop the oil reserves somewhere out there," she said eventually. "Apparently, it wasn't a popular idea. Harry insisted that what was good for America was, in the long run, good for most of the world – you know how Yanks get about these things.

"Well, it got louder and louder, and it's got to be well above *fortissimo* before that sort of thing is even noticed at one of my parties – "

"You're well-known for the decibel level of your *soirées*," Lucinda put in.

"Well, the Arabs got all excited and said they were going to call their embassy and have the whole project stopped. Then, Justin got involved and the argument switched to him. It was just a lot of political nonsense, nothing you should worry about. Just don't invite Arabs to your wedding."

"Harry's dead."

"Well then, you have nothing to worry about," Miranda said.

Lucinda rose, glass in hand and walked to the door.

"Did you know he was dead?" she asked.

"No."

Lucinda opened the door and started out, but stopped.

"Silly me," she said. She shut the door firmly and crossed the room to place the glass she still carried on a small French-polished table.

The bedroom door opened.

Undivulged Crimes

"Is she gone yet?" asked a small Arab girl.

"*No!*" cried Miranda, lunging for the glass before it touched the perfection of the table-top.

We all have our priorities.

Lucinda looked at the odalisque.

"Matching nighties?" she said shaking her head, "That's tacky, Miranda. Good-night."

Lucinda was not a little alarmed by the presence of the Arab girl at Miranda's; not for any social reasons, but because of the link with the bombing of the aeroplane. (Lucinda still thought of them as aeroplanes, a mark, no doubt, of her early education when she was obliged to curtsy whenever giving something to, or accepting something from, a teacher).

So uneasy was she that she took a taxi home.

ల

In the safety of her own flat, Lucinda made herself another gin and tonic. She hoped the Arab girl wasn't a strict Moslem as Miranda was enough to drive anyone to the bottle.

All of a sudden, an uncanny number of Arabs were turning up in her life. She had nothing against them, *per se*, but the whole business was beginning to make her nervous. Hadn't she seen a television play like this where the beneficiary was kidnapped, and the money wrenched from her to finance a military coup? The one thing she was certain of was that she would have to plan her life

The Benefactor

fairly carefully for a while. She would let someone know everything she planned to do in the event that she was suddenly removed from circulation. If only she had a regular boyfriend now. Though, when word of her inheritance got out, she'd have dozens.

The identity of Harold P. Carroll, Jr seemed to be the key. She would visit Justin Southworth in the morning and see what he knew. Chinamend would just have to do without her.

The suddenness of the telephone made her nearly drop her drink. It was Samantha.

"I just wanted to see if you got back from Miranda's safely."

"Yes, just."

"Just got back, or just made it safely?"

"Miranda's pretty hard to take at the best of times," said Lucinda. "That flat's like something from a horror film."

"She let you in?"

"I even sat on the sofa."

"Lucky you."

"Samantha, can you meet me for lunch tomorrow? About one at the Basil Street Hotel?"

"No. It's absolutely impossible," Samantha replied.

"Good, I'll see you then. I'm going to see Justin Southworth in the morning. Miranda said he knew him."

"Who?"

Undivulged Crimes

"Southworth."

"Who knows him?"

"Sam, we all know him. Miranda was right, you do muddle everything. See you at one. Good-night."

༄

Justin Southworth's office was near New Scotland Yard. It was a firm of engineers, so it was not inconceivable that Harry Carroll knew him through some project or other.

"Harold T. Carroll, Jr?" Justin Southworth said, "Never heard of him, love."

"But you had a fight with him at Miranda's party – and the Arabs!"

"Everyone fights at Miranda's. It was just my turn."

"Well, the man you were fighting with was Harold T. Carroll, Jr."

"No, it wasn't."

"Well, who was it, then?" Lucinda asked.

Justin moved across the office and sat behind his rather shabby desk.

"Lucinda, why is this so important that you got me out of a conference?"

"Justin, just tell me who it was you were fighting with, and then you can go back to carving up Arabia with your projects."

"I can't."

The Benefactor

"I thought all engineering companies were carving up Arabia, Persia, the Sudan and all those other sandy places."

"No, I mean I can't tell you who I was arguing with, but it's awfully nice to see you," he said. "Are you doing anything this weekend? A client gave me tickets to the Highland Games in Perth."

"Justin, do you know Harold P. Carroll, Jr?"

"No."

"Will you tell me with whom you were arguing about Arabia at Miranda's party?"

"I can't."

"You don't know who it was?" she demanded.

"I know. I just can't tell you," Justin said.

"You know he's dead."

"Who?"

"What's-his-name. Harold P. Carroll, Jr."

Justin stood and looked out the window.

"So, they got to him."

"Who?"

"I can't tell you. You don't want to know," Justin was finally serious. "Please, Cindy, stay out of it. You can't be all that serious about a semi-wrinkly Yank anyway."

"Whether I am or not is not at issue," she said. "I am trying to find out something about him, and it's all starting to frighten me."

Justin started to move towards her.

Undivulged Crimes

"All I want from you, Southworth, is information, and if you're not going to give it to me, you can get back to your meeting."

Lucinda left before he could reply.

It was not the turn of events that she had expected. In fact, the whole thing was beginning to look decidedly dangerous.

She went to the Basil Street Hotel, but on the way began to feel that she was being followed. She stopped; crossed the street several times under the pretence of looking in shop windows, and even retraced her steps for a hundred yards or more. No one looked particularly suspicious; no one looked particularly harmless.

She entered the hotel and went up to the restaurant. No one would follow her up there, which was why she had chosen it.

Samantha was waiting at a table and had devoured a basket of bread rolls and half a bottle of Chablis.

"How long have you been waiting?"

"About this long," Samantha giggled holding up the bottle.

"How did you get on with Justin? I thought you'd bring him along."

"No chance," Lucinda said sitting down and pouring herself a glass.

"What did he tell you?"

The Benefactor

"That Harry was a spy involved in some sort of clandestine operation. That Harold T. Carroll, Jr wasn't his real name and that he – Justin – was mixed up in it too."

"I didn't think people could be told about such things," Samantha said.

"They can't. I just guessed it," Lucinda admitted. "Justin wouldn't tell me anything, and he seemed rattled when he found that Harry was dead."

"He didn't know?"

"No. Strange, that, isn't it?"

They ordered lunch. Lucinda's appetite had increased with her frustration.

"What are you going to do now?"

"Try the American Embassy."

"They won't tell you anything."

"I know, but if they see me, I'll know that they know what is going on."

Lucinda stood up.

"I'll ring them now – depending on their reaction, I'll know how deeply they're in on it."

࿙

Ringing an embassy was not something that Lucinda did every day, but she knew well in advance that she would be given the run-around. Whom to approach first was critical. She considered demanding to speak to the ambassador himself, but then realised that even his acknowledgement of Harold P. Carroll, Jr. would compromise his position. She thought of playing the dumb blonde and innocently going in to ask for information about the nice man who had died and left her all his money. This had certain advantages, but she didn't think she could carry it off. For one thing, she wasn't blonde.

She dialled the number and threw herself on the mercy of the telephonist, or whatever Americans called them.

"I'd like to know whom to speak to about a matter of national security," she said firmly. Yanks were apt to rise to those key words.

"What is the nature of the business?" the voice asked.

"It is sufficiently important that I won't discuss it with a telephone operator," she said in glacial tones.

"I assure you I have a security clearance," the operator replied in a surprisingly unflapped manner.

"Nevertheless, I shan't tell you. It's about something I stumbled on accidentally, and I'd like to know what to do."

"That would be Mr Jaraslaw Zynckiwicki."

"Who?"

"Just call him Mr Zee."

"You can't be serious," Lucinda said, but the call had been transferred.

"Zynckiwicki," said the telephone officially.

The Benefactor

"Can you put me on to Harold T. Carroll's control, please," Lucinda said sweetly, very glad that she had been watching *Smiley's People*.

There was an audible gasp at the embassy end of the line, but Lucinda was undaunted.

"Who is this?" Zynckiwicki asked, trying to be calm.

"My name is Lucinda Lord."

"And did you know Mr Carroll?"

"Only slightly."

"Well enough to be one of his beneficiaries, though," Zynckiwicki prompted.

"And what do you mean by that?" she asked.

Lucinda heard a click on the line.

"Are you having this call traced? If so, you're using rather noisy equipment. If it's not you, I think we're being monitored, too. Shall I call back?"

"No, Miss Lord. We're tracing the call."

"Why don't you just ask me for my address?"

"Well," Zynckiwicki began in a rather embarrassed tone, "We're not supposed to ask for addresses of callers of the opposite sex. It's regarded as improper."

"But tracing calls is all right?"

"Perfectly."

"Well, can I have the name of Mr Carroll's control?"

"Now Miss Lord, you know I can't give you that information."

Undivulged Crimes

"Oh, I know. But I have to stay on the line for three minutes for you to be able to trace it, don't I?"

"About that," came the grudging reply.

"Well, I can't think of much else to say."

"Perhaps you could tell me how you met Mr Carroll."

"At a party, for about half an hour. It was at Miranda's. You know Miranda, don't you?"

"I can't tell you that."

"Well, if you don't ask me about her, I shall assume you do."

"Fair enough."

"Would you believe me if I said I didn't know anything about Harold T. Carroll, Jr?"

"It's not likely."

"I didn't think so, but suppose – "

"Just a minute, Miss Lord. We've got the trace now. You live at 32 Smith Terrace, Chelsea, SW1."

"SW3, actually. Apartment 4."

"Quite."

"Thank you, Mr Sinkowitz."

"Zynkiwicki."

"Quite."

Lucinda rang off, quite pleased with herself.

ଔ

Samantha and Lucinda dragged their bags to the counter at Heathrow's Terminal Three.

The Benefactor

"I don't see how you can face the possibility of flying after all that's gone on in the past week," Samantha said.

"I didn't think I could cope either," said Lucinda. "But now, I'm certain I'm perfectly safe."

"I hope so. I've been looking forward to this trip for weeks. But what makes you so certain that you're safe. After all, just about everyone involved will become alarmed when they realise you've gone to Dubai."

"That's why I rang the Yanks," Lucinda said.

"I still don't get it," Samantha said, heaving her suitcase onto the scales.

"The Arabs have been following me, you know."

"Yes."

"Well, after my phone call to the embassy, the Americans are following me as well. I'm counting on them to run interference."

"Did you tell them you were going to Dubai to visit your father?"

"Of course not. Do you think they'd believe he was British Consul out there?" Lucinda asked.

"No."

"Neither did I. So, on the whole, I thought it was the best thing to do."

"I don't know what you've been reading lately, Cindy, but one of these days you'll get yourself into a lot of trouble."

"I'll worry about that then."

Undivulged Crimes

They left the ticket counter and headed for the gate.

"Oh, just a minute, Sam. This needs one final touch."

Lucinda went to a forlorn little counter in the corner of the terminal.

"What's the maximum insurance one can purchase?" she asked.

"Five hundred thousand pounds."

"Of course, silly me."

"May I have two policies for two hundred fifty thousand each, please?"

Lucinda filled in the forms quickly and paid the fee.

"I hope you're not expecting the worst!" Samantha protested. "I'm flying with you!"

"No, but this way I won't mind."

"Why? What have you done, Lord?"

"I just took out two policies for my friends. One for Nigel Woodstock and one for Jaraslaw Zynckiwicki."

"You devious beast."

The Remarkable Adventure of the Royal Society

Undivulged Crimes

The Remarkable Adventure of the Royal Society

One day, I suppose, this unpublished note about an incident in the life of Sherlock Holmes will be "discovered," (though it is in plain sight in my working notebooks) and hailed as a "lost case."

Of course, it's not a case at all; merely an amusing anecdote, bereft of theft, blackmail, or murder. I hope that if it does appear, it will entertain the readers of the future in the way the actual event entertained those who were involved.

J.H.W.

Undivulged Crimes

The Remarkable Adventure of the Royal Society

Though neither Sherlock nor his brother Mycroft had many they could number as friends, they had a very wide circle of acquaintance. Sherlock's circle was wider and of greater social depth than Mycroft's; Mycroft's were certainly more powerful, and more international.

Readers of my record of the exploits of Sherlock Holmes will know that neither he nor his brother were what today are called "joiners." Mycroft had his membership of the Diogenes Club, of which he had been a founder, but I never knew Sherlock to be a member of any organisation. However, in my experience, I also never knew him to be forbidden entry to even the most exclusive establishments on Pall Mall.

While essentially self-absorbed in their own worlds, the Holmes brothers' interests were extraordinarily wide. Sherlock regularly subscribed to expeditions, supported research, and made contributions to the advancement of science. I suspect Mycroft did the same. This suspicion was reinforced by the fact that enterprising young men at various organisations and charities regularly proposed money-raising activities involving both Sherlock and

Undivulged Crimes

Mycroft. Often, these were framed as a challenge of some sort, setting brother against brother for the attention such a contest would receive in the press, thereby bolstering the chances of rich rewards for the beneficiary organisation.

Needless to say, all of these proposals were consigned to the rubbish or fire.

Yet, one damp afternoon when I called at 221B Baker Street in the hope of some tea and civilised conversation (not to mention a smoke, which Mary had lately forbidden in our home), I found Sherlock pondering a letter. He set it aside when I came in, and it wasn't until I was buttering the last scone that he mentioned it.

"Watson, I have received another fund-raising proposal involving Mycroft and me in a duel of wits," he began.

"But you always throw them away," I said.

"This one is a little more intriguing," he replied, "and worth a bit more consideration."

At this, he fell silent for about five minutes, during which he finished his tea and filled and lit his pipe. Only when he was satisfied that the pipe was properly lit and drawing satisfactorily did he speak.

"The Royal Geographical Society is proposing an expedition to the South Pole," he said. "You may have read of it; it's in the papers. There was an idea that it might be

The Remarkable Adventure of the Royal Society

fitting to reach the pole on the first of January 1900, so there is ample preparation time."

Indeed, I had read of the proposal to take a dozen ships and launch an attack on the pole from three different landing sites simultaneously. Not only would that strategy increase the likelihood of success, but also create the excitement of a competition that might sustain public interest for the duration of the journey.

"It's a cunning plan, and encourages interest and public support," he continued. "This letter takes the plan a stage further. The Royal Geographical Society has entered talks with the Royal Society to encourage the development of scientific equipment that might be used on the expedition. A thousand useful instruments for measuring, tracking, recording and preserving. Everything is covered from food and drink, to ink that won't freeze. Warm clothing, photographic equipment, means of improving navigation and the cladding of vessels for protection against the ice. Portable heaters, prefabricated buildings, ice cutters and goggles!"

Seldom had I seen Holmes so stimulated by anything he had not thought of. It was a magnificent quest, making the most of the ingenuity of the Empire, and for the practical purpose of the eventual settlement of Antarctica.

"While this is a very preliminary letter, it is soliciting my support in helping to launch a large number of individual private projects to raise money to fund the

Undivulged Crimes

research and development of all the scientific and survival equipment required," he said, and added, "And, I am inclined to help them!"

I very nearly spilled jam on my waistcoat to hear this accession to the idea and wondered in what way he would offer his support.

"Come! Let us set about putting things in motion!" he exclaimed and threw off his smoking jacket.

He had slipped into his boots and wrapped his coat about him and was on the landing, heading to the stairs, by the time I wiped my fingers and stood up. By the time I reached him on the pavement, he had hailed a cab.

"The Diogenes Club!"

I was thrown back into the seat as the hansom accelerated towards Saint James. When I recovered myself, I looked at Holmes who was rubbing the palms of his hands together before his face and grinning.

"Are you involving Mycroft in this?" I inquired.

For a moment, I thought he had not heard me, but he turned to me, and said darkly:

"Oh, Mycroft is deeply involved in this already."

He was silent for the rest of the journey and it wasn't until we'd been admitted to the Strangers' Room that he spoke again.

Mycroft was there, consulting his watch when we entered.

"You are seventeen minutes late," Mycroft said.

The Remarkable Adventure of the Royal Society

"I would have been on time had not Watson decided to have a third scone," he replied.

"I hope it was good," Mycroft said in my direction. He seldom spoke to me direct, preferring me to overhear what he said to his brother.

"You have received a letter from the Royal Geographical Society?" Holmes asked.

"I have," Mycroft replied.

"Of course, you have! This whole project has The Diogenes Club written all over it. I suspect India is sucking up all the Government's money and rather than raise taxes, this scheme between the geographers and the scientists was cooked up to fill the void," Holmes said.

"It's not a complete void," Mycroft replied.

It was characteristic of these two never to vary their tone, pitch or inflection. They might declare war on each other in the same voice they would request the other to pass the mustard. I put it down to laziness on Mycroft's part; he was never known to exert himself except to clip the end of a cigar if no one was around to do it for him. For the mercurial Sherlock, I attributed his forbearance either to brotherly deference, or to a determination not to let Mycroft see him as anything other than unflappable. Whatever the reason, and it was probably a combination of both, it was the way they invariably communicated.

Undivulged Crimes

Mycroft indicated that we might sit down, but no refreshment was offered.

"I have to tell you, Mycroft, that this is an excellent project, worthy of the dawn of a new century. Ten years is a good period for the necessary preparations," Holmes said. "But how will you keep the interest going all that time, and maintain the flow of investment?"

"A good question, Sherlock," his brother replied. "What is proposed is a series of annual prizes for the developments thus far. Details of the inventions and the awards ceremony will be of sufficient interest for the press, and the scientific community will be involved with the scrutiny of the objects and ideas. A final selection of what to take on the expedition itself will not be made until a year before it sets out."

"Giving time for scrutiny and testing," Holmes commented. "Very thorough, Mycroft."

"Thank you."

At this point, both gentlemen paused in their conversation and stared into space for several minutes, leaving me to feel like an unwanted chaperone. Eventually, Sherlock spoke again.

"This proposed competition between us," he began. "Was this of your design, too? I thought it too carefully proposed to be the work of a geographer, and far too subtle to be the writing of a scientist. The inferences, tone

The Remarkable Adventure of the Royal Society

and veiled deprecation suggest the mind of a diplomatist."

"I'm glad we still understand each other," Mycroft said.

Sherlock nodded, and considered his next question.

"How far has your thinking gone as to the nature of our competition?" he asked.

"I think I have it fully mapped out," Mycroft replied.

"The Napoleon of subterfuge," Holmes said, then turned to me. "Napoleon had two great abilities. His first was that he could look at a map and see the landscape in his mind well enough to plan his battle. Where to place cannon; where to launch the cavalry charge from, and how to use the infantry to maximum advantage.

"His second ability was to be able to visualise a battle so clearly that he could calculate what he would need to win, down to the last six cannon balls. My brother has a similar talent when it comes to matters of persuasion and deceit."

Interesting though this genteel sparring was, I was thinking that a glass of sherry or madeira would be acceptable about now. Unfortunately, there remained no sign of either.

Holmes' gaze returned to his brother.

The two regarded each other for a few moments when Sherlock spoke again.

Undivulged Crimes

"I see," he said, and then turned to me again. "He's not going to tell me, Watson. I'm going to have to work this out for myself, and for his entertainment and yours. Perhaps, Mycroft, you may at least order us some sherry to give some mutuality to the entertainment. It's been at least an hour since Watson finished his tea."

As Mycroft signalled for the butler, Holmes began his speculations.

"This is to be a duel between two brothers, one slightly better known than the other, but both regarded as colourful, if unexciting, characters. In order to achieve the goals of press attention and success in raising awareness and money for the venture, this will have to be some event carried out in public – and one that the public will understand. So, Watson, solving cryptographic ciphers wouldn't be suitable.

"We can't stage a murder to solve; well, at least we can't be seen to stage a murder; and, although a grand and colourful occasion and suited for large crowds, a horse race would be suitable for neither of us. Rattling sabres or rapiers wouldn't do either, for the same athletic reasons; and while a pistol duel is more sedentary, marksmanship was never one of Mycroft's accomplishments."

"It only became one of yours because you didn't have to compete against me," Mycroft said.

Holmes ignored the remark, and continued thinking out loud.

The Remarkable Adventure of the Royal Society

"We are both known for our powers of deduction, and our cerebral abilities. I am known as a decent boxer and fighter in various oriental styles, but, alas, Mycroft is not. A scavenger hunt would draw on our reasoning, but would be impossible for the public to follow; that leaves the more conventional games.

"Whist requires four people, and card games depend as much on luck as on skill, so they would not do, which leaves – "

There was a moment's silence, then Holmes gave a rich laugh.

"Oh, very good, Mycroft. In fact, perfect, and I fully approve!"

He stood up and headed to the door.

"Well done, Mycroft! I shall look forward to it! Come, Watson!"

I rose, as puzzled as I had been all afternoon.

"Just let me know the time and place, Mycroft."

"Time and place for what?" I asked, hoping to regain contact with reality.

"My brother has conceived the ideal field of battle for us: a chess board!"

With that, he turned and bounded out of the room, nearly colliding with the butler with the tray of glasses and decanter of sherry.

03

Undivulged Crimes

Weeks went by in the development and promoting of the event. The newspapers expressed strong opinions on who would win; they published details of the expedition; the planned competition categories for inventions; suggestions on how the chess match should be played; how the venue should be arranged, and even details of the authorised bookmakers for the battle of the brothers.

Several of the largest bookmakers had formed a consortium with the consent of the sponsoring societies to take bets on the outcome of the game. Unusually, 80 per cent of the money collected would be given to the two societies with the winners dividing 15 per cent. The bookmakers would split the remainder.

While Sherlock attracted more bets, they were of smaller amounts, whereas Mycroft had fewer but wealthier backers, so the money raised by each – published daily – was roughly equal.

Journalists called at Baker Street on an almost daily basis, and Mrs Hudson was obliged to engage her sister-in-law, Maude, to answer the door and send away reporters who tried to gain access after Holmes' business hours. He and Mycroft had agreed not to give any interviews until a week before the match.

In the newspapers, there was much to-ing and fro-ing about where the event was to be held. Grand schemes were proposed to hold the event in important public places. Many of the papers offered space in their own

The Remarkable Adventure of the Royal Society

buildings. Other proposals were to hold it in the Albert Hall, or at the Crystal Palace, but few showed any interest in going to Sydenham.

Seeing the advantage of not disclosing the agreed venue, the Royal Geographical Society and the Royal Society were able to keep the discussion going for several weeks.

While Holmes and his brother exchanged frequent messages, presumably about the format, rules, formality and otherwise, of the forthcoming match, they did not meet. On more than one occasion, I offered to play a few games with Holmes, but he declined.

During this time, he undertook several cases and travelled outside London, sometimes for several days in pursuit of solving them. While visiting these different towns, he was, predictably, asked whether he could beat Mycroft, how good his chess game actually was, and what his favourite opening moves were.

I read several of the reports and Holmes appears to have been unusually accommodating. Though he never answered those questions, he did promote the expedition and the challenges it presented to the men undertaking it. He spoke about the competitions for equipment and these conversations earned a gratifying number of column inches.

Three weeks before the event, more than ten thousand pounds had been wagered with the authorised

Undivulged Crimes

bookmakers, and many thousands more collected through public subscription.

"Holmes, aren't you going to do any practising?" I asked in desperation one afternoon.

"Do you not think I am busy enough, Watson?" he asked.

"Yes, but when was the last time you played Mycroft?"

He considered this.

"When I was fourteen. He fianchettoed both his bishops and then attacked before I'd worked out how to combat his formations."

"And you haven't played him since?" I asked incredulously.

"I calculated that leaving him with a false sense of superiority would eventually become an advantage for me," he replied. "And, you see, it has."

"No, I *don't* see that it has," I protested, wondering if Holmes had ever got to the bottom of the Zukertort Opening.

"You worry too much, Watson," he said, reaching for his tobacco. "Don't worry; I know how my brother's mind works."

Holmes endured a lot of cheeky ribbing during this period as well as a flood of post containing suggestions and diagrams of how he might be assured of victory.

It was curious to see how, even in this, the breadth of the human condition was reflected. There were those

The Remarkable Adventure of the Royal Society

who wrote with simple wishes for good luck, saying that at one point Holmes had helped them, and they wished to help him. Myriad suggestions of opening moves were received. Complex diagrams working out the astrological charts of both Holmes and Mycroft showing how the moon would favour a Queen's Gambit, or a Grünfeld Defence, while other writers would insist that the Sicilian Defence or some other curious move would be the only one to lead to victory.

I believed that his best hope was in a Kandahar Gambit, which was popular during my army days, but the reception that Holmes gave the suggestions led me to keep my thoughts to myself. The most I could get him to say was, "The winner will be determined with the choosing of the pawn."

I regarded this cryptic remark as a smoke screen, but as events unfolded, I recognised the truth of what my friend had said.

Every cabby in London offered Sherlock a strategy. I thought some of them remarkably shrewd, but Holmes, having proffered warm thanks, promptly forgot them.

"The good old English Opening," was Inspector Lestrade's suggestion. "Can't go wrong with that; it would be unpatriotic to use anything different."

"Not even the Victoria Variation?" Holmes asked, mischievously.

Undivulged Crimes

Lestrade was silent until he acknowledged to himself that either he didn't know it, or he was being had.

"A chess match is no frivolous thing," he said when he spoke again. "Especially one that is the focus of so much attention. The public deserves a good show, and so do the Empire's chess players."

Holmes rounded on Lestrade and for a moment the inspector looked as though he feared Holmes might hit him. In the event, Holmes smiled.

"My dear Lestrade, you are absolutely right," he said. "I can promise you, and the Empire's chess players that this will be a match that will be talked about for decades."

Lestrade recovered his composure, gave himself a slight shake, and returned Holmes' friendly tone.

"I hope so, sir," he said. "But, I suppose the really important thing is the success of the Great Expedition."

"Once again, old friend, you are absolutely right," said Holmes.

Having twice heard sentences he'd never thought he'd hear the great detective utter, he bade us good night and left.

Holmes chuckled.

"You really shouldn't do that, Holmes," I said. "It's hardly fair."

"Quite right, Watson, but Mycroft and I do seem to have created something of a monster. Still, as the

The Remarkable Adventure of the Royal Society

admirable Lestrade said, it's not really about Mycroft and me; it's about the Great Expedition!"

☙

September came and with it the week of the "showdown," as our American cousins say, between Sherlock and Mycroft Holmes. There had been something of a lull in the betting and contributions during the slack weeks of August following the bank holiday, but interest returned at the beginning of September when it was announced that the competition would be held in the main lecture hall of the Royal Society.

There would be 100 seats and 300 standing places. Two giant chess boards were being constructed with moveable pieces. One of them would hang in the lecture hall, and one outside so the public could follow the match. A steward would move pieces that hung on the board with a stick, much as a croupier might move counters and plaques. A message would be relayed to another steward out of doors who would replicate the move.

To ensure that as many of the public had access to the event to which many had subscribed, the standing places were to be allocated by ballot. For five shillings, anyone could apply to either organising society and have their names entered in a draw. The seats would be sold by a closed auction. Bids, in guineas, would be submitted and all the bids recorded in the order of the amount. Starting from the highest, seats would be allocated at the price

Undivulged Crimes

level where all seats were sold. This ensured a relative consensus of price while filling the seats.

Mycroft and Sherlock appeared together at Rules to enjoy a meal a few weeks before the match. Having enjoyed a good meal and several bottles affably, they fell into a very loud, long and public dispute about who would supply the chess set to be played with. To all but the greatest dolt, this was obviously a manufactured farce designed for the press, which willingly obliged, giving the dispute much coverage.

As if providentially, two days later, an emissary from the Imperial Chess Club of Calcutta arrived with a handsome mahogany Staunton set of pieces and a highly-polished board with fine inlay and moulding. Both men visited the Royal Society to inspect the set and thank the representative and the chess club.

The newspapers hardly needed this synthetic and readily-resolved spat as they were running a stream of stories. There were interviews with the presidents of both societies, with members of the admiralty that would ultimately be supplying the ships, and with leading chess players. Stores reported that chess sets had sold out and were being re-sold at a premium.

The government, which was dealing with some very perplexing issues at the time was glad of the distraction. This titbit was not in the papers, but came via Mycroft. Indeed, he joked that several cabinet ministers were

The Remarkable Adventure of the Royal Society

preparing to make substantial personal donations to the expedition in gratitude.

There were other stratagems to ensure that the public kept talking about the match and the expedition fund. Mycroft and Sherlock carried on barbed correspondence in all the London newspapers. Mycroft would write to the *Globe* saying that the table they sat at should be square; Sherlock would reply in the *Star* that it could only be rectangular; Mycroft announced in the Pall Mall *Gazette* that he wanted the table on a Persian rug, while Sherlock would stipulate in St James's *Gazette* that it should be Turkish, and so on in the *Evening News Standard*, *Echo*, and then back to the *Globe*, *Times*, *Telegraph*, and the rest. They argued about whether they should have drinks, and if so what; what level of evening wear they should appear in; whether medals should be worn; and, what make of chess clock should be used.

No doubt there will be future readers who for some reason have come to believe that the Victorian Age was a dull one, but I can assure them that it was not. It was an age of great excitement and achievement; it was also an age of great genius and equally great folly. How the Royal Society Chess Match of Friday, 23 September 1892 will be regarded in the future – if, indeed, it is even remembered – is left to the seeds of time.

On the night, it was almost impossible to enter Carlton House Terrace. Crowds and carriages pushed down

Undivulged Crimes

the cul-de-sac, and surged up the steps from the Mall and down from Pall Mall and Waterloo Place.

As it was important that both Mycroft and Sherlock were seen arriving, a large contingent of the Metropolitan Police was needed to ensure their progress. Their arrival was coordinated so that Mycroft was at the doorway waving to the crowd when Sherlock's cab pulled up. The two met, shook hands, and waved again before disappearing inside.

Stewards then arrived to hang the large chess board and arrange its pieces. Torches and flambeaux illuminated the board as the dusk settled in, enhancing the sense of drama.

Once inside, the two men wasted little time in getting down to business. The President of the Royal Society read out the agreed rules, and the President of the Royal Geographical Society picked a black and white pawn from the board, turned his back to the Holmeses, and then held out his closed, gloved fists.

As agreed, Mycroft being the elder, tapped the President's left hand which opened to reveal a white pawn. Mycroft took it and placed it on the board and Sherlock did likewise. As the two faced each other, the President had one last function, he moved behind the table so that he was facing the audience. Between the players there appeared to be two clocks on a see-saw-like mechanism. This was the Thomas B. Wilson chess clock – agreed upon

The Remarkable Adventure of the Royal Society

by Sherlock and Mycroft after much debate – that would measure the amount of time each player had left to play. The President pushed the side nearest Sherlock down to activate Mycroft's clock.

The silence of that great hall was such that it could be heard ticking in all corners. And it ticked, and ticked and ticked.

Mycroft studied the board for nearly a full five minutes. (Had he not had months to consider a first move?) He then paused and took a drink of the port that was next to him, dabbed his mouth with a linen handkerchief, and thought some more.

After six minutes, he made his move.

Pawn to King's Bishop 4.

Mycroft pushed his clock down to start Sherlock's.

A ripple of applause was heard as the steward made the move on the giant board, and the softest murmuring could be heard for several seconds. This was followed by applause from outside the building, and a good deal more discussion before quiet was restored.

Sherlock stared at the board. Then, he leaned back in his chair, tipping it onto its back legs. Then he brought his hands together, almost prayerfully before his mouth. He then suddenly stood, nearly knocking his chair over, causing a gasp from the audience. He regarded his pieces, and then walked around the whole table before sitting down again. His hands came together again and then . . . .

Undivulged Crimes

And then, indeed.

Holmes, slowly and deliberately moved his hand to his king and toppled it. The small noise echoed around the room like thunder. He fell back in his chair for an instant, before rising again, and extending his hand to his brother.

"An extraordinary coup."

My heart sank. What had I just witnessed? The whole assembly appeared to be asking itself the same question. Was this genius, or folly? In those moments, no one seemed able to decide.

In one of the few spontaneous actions of my life (which included one that resulted in being shot in Afghanistan, and the other that resulted in my marriage to Mary; the fact that both had lifetime consequences did not escape me in those few seconds), I stood up, shouted "Bravo!" and began to applaud.

Thank heavens for the English upper-class mentality; it perceives itself as leaders, but in reality, loves to be led, and within an instant, the whole hall was cheering the Holmes brothers to the echo.

Outside, things were a little more realistic. Once the police had cleared the streets to enable those within to go home, there were rocks and bottles strewn about, a large number of broken windows, and a few fires of debris still burning. There was nothing extraordinary about the dead horse.

The Remarkable Adventure of the Royal Society

☙

Whether the chess match between Sherlock and Mycroft was an example of great genius or great folly, history will tell. Personally, I regard it as a masterstroke of public manipulation. It created a sensation for weeks, attracting attention and money to a worthy cause. The obvious collusion between the brothers kept the letters and editorial pages full for a further six weeks. Several people tried suing the bookmakers' consortium, but as there was no evidence that the result was fixed, and there was a clear winner, no action could be taken. Indeed, the result wasn't fixed, as it rested with the random choice of the pawn, so neither Sherlock nor Mycroft, on entering the Royal Society, knew what the outcome would be.

The event itself raised nearly 7,400 guineas, and the public donations and subscriptions came to another £141,000 and continue to be collected.

The three of us dined a week later, when it was safe to go out again. Rules was judged a suitable place as its upstairs dining room offered some safety from the street, and the food was acceptable.

When Mycroft had tasted and accepted the claret, I raised my glass.

"To the Holmes brothers, whose showmanship in the past months rivalled D'Oyly-Carte's. To a masterpiece of theatre!"

Undivulged Crimes

Both Sherlock and Mycroft looked decidedly embarrassed, even sheepish. They looked at each other as though they were school boys caught in some compromising activity.

"Watson," Sherlock began, but was cut off by Mycroft.

"Dr Watson," he said quietly. "It is to you we owe the success of our little plan."

He raised his glass.

"Indeed, John," Sherlock said. "Had you not begun to applaud, someone was bound to boo, and that would have been disaster. In those silent seconds, I knew it was a grave error not to bring you in on our plan. There is no doubt you saved the day, and quite possibly our skins."

At this time, I don't know if the Great Expedition ever went ahead, and if it did, if it met with success. If it did not, then it wasn't for want of effort of Sherlock and Mycroft Holmes.

So, there, reader, you have it: The Remarkable Adventure of the Royal Society. I call it remarkable, for in what other story do Inspector Lestrade and I receive a compliment from the great consulting detective?

The Pit

Undivulged Crimes

The Pit

Norman Dodge was surprised that he hadn't thought of it before.

The small Oxfordshire farm had been his home all his life, but the idea had never occurred to him.

Norman Dodge always felt he needed some outside interest. His work at Cowley was sedentary and not especially challenging. Accounting wasn't the sort of work to take home with you. Indeed, taking the Leyland books home with him would have got him into serious trouble.

He wasn't one for spending evenings down at the local, though he enjoyed a pint now and again; nor was he one to take up stamp collecting. Since they had ceased working the family farm, which wasn't much to begin with, he had nothing to occupy his mind after work. The good fields were leased to a neighbouring dairyman, but the three acres around the house had lain fallow for a long time.

He kept a small plot for strawberries, and there were roses around the house, but the rest of the land was just sitting there. Norman Dodge knew that farming it would be a full-time job and that nothing good would come without that full-time commitment.

Undivulged Crimes

Now that he was alone he felt the emptiness of the house and the uselessness of the land more than ever. However, this new idea would be fun. It would be active, healthy and challenging. Granted, he would not be able to work at it all year round, but there were other related activities he could engage in. The plan, as he saw it, was to search for archaeological remains. The Romans had been all over Oxfordshire, and during the middle ages, there had been much farming in the area.

It was April, and the days were lengthening, and he could dig after work. The research could wait until rainy weekends or even until the autumn. After all, he didn't want to look for anything, he just wanted to find something – it didn't really matter what.

Even so, he knew he couldn't be completely haphazard about it. He knew that the Romans frequently built kilns on the tops of small hills. He had walked through newly ploughed fields and seen the reddish shards of broken pots in the gaping furrows. He had seen crude splinters of green glass, even the odd bit of shapeless bronze. They never held any interest for him. He'd never picked one up; never read a book about Roman Oxfordshire; never visited the Roman section of the Ashmolean.

That evening, after supper, he walked the boundaries of his land, except for the part leased to the dairyman, which, in any event, was across the road.

The Pit

He knew the land well. He had worked it as a boy – but as a boy not interested in farming.

That evening, the land looked different to him. It wasn't just the farm his father had bought after moving down from Lancashire in time for the war. It was old land. Ancient land.

There was a swell, not a hill really, which tipped gracefully towards the small stream which cut across the property before passing through a culvert under the road and wandering across the pasture. The perfect site for a kiln, or even a villa, he thought. He continued surveying the land more closely than he had ever done. There were no old walls. . . but there might have been; there were no eighteenth-century ha-has that he could see; there were no old wells. . . that he knew of. The possibilities were endless.

He considered the house itself. There was nothing remarkable about that.

It was a late Victorian building which had started life as a cottage and been added to over the years. Even now, it was only six rooms with a collection of sheds and rotting loose boxes. He had already begun to knock them down for firewood. They were not old, he knew. But had there been another house there before?

An inspection of the foundations indicated that they were no older than the house. He was realistic about it. He had never heard any stories about the house or the farm. It was near nothing of any interest except the pub which had been a coaching inn. Finding out the details of the land could be done at the library some wet winter afternoon.

No medieval sites were near, either. Supposedly there had been a priory a mile or so away. The story was that it had been dismantled, stone by stone, and used in the building of one of the Oxford colleges. Occasionally there were attempts to fix its former location, but no one had found any evidence of its existence.

This, he thought, was another possibility. What fun to turn up something the scholars hadn't been able to find.

Then, there was the possibility of some Anglo-Saxon remains. They had been great farmers. Even now it was possible to see the gouges in the land of their long narrow allotments; the embankments along their roads; even some of their hedgerows still were in existence.

Yes, Saxon ruins were a possibility; though, except for churches, few Saxon buildings survived. Still, Norman Dodge did not rule out such a discovery.

Having completed the tour of the property, he went to the small barn, which still stood near the house. He rooted about for a while before emerging with a sledge hammer and some old wooden fence posts. He had intended them for the fire, since they had rotted off at

The Pit

ground level, but he decided they would serve his new purpose.

He carried them to the crown of the little hill. Then, standing at the very top of the rise, he took the sledge and one post about thirty feet from the top and proceeded to drive the post into the spongy ground. Even with its blunted end, the post was quickly driven a foot into the earth. He repeated the process until he had marked out a large square encompassing the hill top.

This, he thought, is where I shall dig.

The light had faded, and Norman Dodge returned to the house and thought.

Unusually for him, work dragged the next day. He was eager to begin the spade work. On odd bits of rough paper, he found himself doodling, a habit which he deplored in others, and had never before been guilty of himself.

He was trying to puzzle out the best way of moving the earth, so that carting it would be the least possible effort. He knew that if he began in the middle, he would have to move the earth the furthest; if he worked around the perimeter, he would have to transport it across the area he had already dug. Moving in regular slices seemed to be the best idea, but it would also be the slowest.

He had seen television films about digging trenches across the length and breadth of a site and elected to do that. While musing on this possibility, it also occurred to

Undivulged Crimes

him that he should sift the earth, too. He couldn't just heap shovelfuls into a wheel barrow and dump it.

He didn't want to miss a clue.

By the time it was five o'clock, Norman Dodge hadn't finished the quarterly reports, but he knew how he wanted to dig.

Within half an hour of leaving work, Norman Dodge was in the field with a shovel, a frame of chicken wire for sifting and a wheel barrow.

Gripping the shovel, he took a deep breath and plunged it into the soft earth. His arms shuddered as the steel shook against an underground rock.

For five minutes, Dodge worked the shovel round the rock and eventually prised it loose.

He bent down and took it in his hands and lifted it. Black, wet earth was pressed into his jacket. He cradled the rock with one arm while brushing the dirt from it with his hand. The next day he'd remember to bring an old scrubbing brush for cleaning such rocks.

Turning the stone, he searched for any sign that it might have been cut. Eventually, he acknowledged that what he had was an ancient, but ordinary, chunk of Oxfordshire.

This presented him with a further problem: he hadn't thought of large rocks and was at a loss for a place to put it.

The Pit

He carried it down to the stream, thinking that if there were going to be many rocks, he'd used them to shore up the banks where they were particularly soft.

He dropped it into the water and pushed it against the bank with the shovel. If nothing else, he thought, I can build an attractive wall along the stream.

It was a good idea, he thought, and returned to his digging.

He found no more large rocks that day, but sifted five barrow-loads of earth. He dumped the rich earth in a mound at the foot of the hill, and dumped the pebbles and smaller stones in a separate pile nearby.

If nothing else, accountancy had taught Norman Dodge to be methodical.

At the end of the day's digging, he had cut a trench one-foot-deep eight feet toward the hilltop. He felt tired, but pleased.

The next morning, he felt dreadful. He hadn't done so much physical work since he was at school. Getting dressed was an enormous effort, and at work that day, his aching back banished any thoughts of digging from his mind.

He did not doodle.

Although tired and sore, he returned to the hill. He dug nine feet that day. He found nothing interesting, but had added the important step of washing the pebbles and checking them more carefully before dumping them. He did this in a plastic bucket of water, filled in the stream. It was slow and rather inefficient, he thought.

At work the next day, he set about solving the problem. He decided to save all the pebbles in the bucket and wash them all at once in the barn with the old pump. That afternoon, he did not dig as much, but he had set an old drinking trough under the pump so that water would wash the stone before flowing down to the drain in the centre of the floor. His set-up reminded him of the sluice-boxes he's seen in western movies about gold-mining. Pebbles rolled down the trough under his inspecting fingers and fell into a small garden sieve and the water ran off.

Very efficient; but he didn't find anything.

Still, he was pleased. The system was working; he was underway. Every evening he worked. He increased his quota as the evenings lengthened to ten loads. The work was methodical and he didn't hurry. At the end of the evening, he would wash the stones and then dump them.

He had found a few things, but not the sort of thing he had hoped to find. There were the remains of several cases of clay pigeons, which only when he found them had he remembered.

When he was about seven, his father had taken to skeet shooting, although that was a grand name for it. At first, farm hands would fling the discs into the sky. Then,

The Pit

one of them had rigged up a catapult from a broken fan belt. They would launch them from behind the crest of the hill and old Dodge would let fly. The sport had lasted the better part of the summer, but was abandoned when the harvest, such as it was, began.

Norman Dodge remembered those evenings as he sifted the clay shards.

He had found a horse shoe – no surprise on a farm – and also a handful of old (but not very old) nails; the remains of a broken cup – of the same pattern still in the kitchen; and a lost spanner.

This did not disappoint him. He had not dug down more than a foot, though by now, the entire hilltop had been excavated.

Having removed the top foot of earth, Norman Dodge found that he had a new problem. He would have to construct a ramp for the wheel barrow to bring it into the pit. At first, he used boards, but he knew that was a temporary solution. It wasn't deep enough yet to use block and tackle with buckets.

He pondered this as he washed the evening's stones. He was intrigued with the idea of digging a downward spiral so he could wheel the barrow upwards.

The next day, he found himself doodling again. He was pleased with himself. He didn't expect to dig further down than about eight feet – if there was nothing there, there was nothing there. Following the perimeter, he

Undivulged Crimes

could drop two feet on each side and have a gradual ramp to the bottom. He could excavate the middle in strips as he went along.

There was no rush now. The digging was therapeutic. He dug as others jogged: it felt good, and he needed to do it. But how much more exciting than jogging, he thought. There was a potential in his digging which did not, could not, exist in mere running.

By July, he had dug nearly four feet down. The ramps on two sides of the pit were complete and in use. They held their shape and were now hard in the warm summer air. Norman Dodge looked forward to his vacation. He would not go away this year, but move twenty-five or thirty loads of earth a day. If it rained, there was still the research to do.

His friends and neighbours watched the hilltop disappear and watched the piles of sifted earth and stone grow. He had told them what he was doing, and they were mildly amused, but none of them had known of anyone ever living in the area before.

Throughout his vacation, he stuck to his programme of digging. He was thrilled with the notion that the very earth he uncovered had lain hidden for perhaps thousands of years.

He was down eight feet. He decided to increase the steepness of the ramp so that each one dropped three

The Pit

feet instead of two. This was still gradual enough to move up without difficulty.

On the last day of his vacation, as luck would have it, while he was washing the stones - which had become larger now – he noticed one with an odd shape.

He put it aside until he had finished washing and discarding the others, then took it into the house where he scrubbed it in the sink.

There was no doubt in his mind: this one had been worked by hand. Three decisive parallel gouges appeared on its side, crude, to be sure, but definitely there.

Norman Dodge took the stone into his sitting room and sat in his over- stuffed chair and switched on his reading lamp.

Through a magnifying glass he studied the small, oval rock and examined the gouges. It was their regularity which to him indicated that they were man-made. But, by whom and when?

To have been buried at that depth, he reckoned, it must have been five to ten thousand years ago. As to whom, Norman Dodge had not the faintest idea. Pre-Celtic, pre-Druid, pre-historic. After contemplating the rock, he found an adhesive label and wrote on it:

Little Mittering Dig, Find No. 1
Norman Dodge, Esq.

Undivulged Crimes

He put the date then pressed the label on to the stone. He then cleared a space on the mantle and placed it there.

He did not want to go to work the next day, but he went. He did not doodle that day, but he did daydream. He thought he should begin to write up the dig, now that it looked like he was about to find things.

During his lunch hour, he bought a small blue notebook with good quality pages and a stitched binding. During the afternoon, he entered a heading, drew a sketch of the farm indicating the position of the pit and at the top of the first clean page wrote "Find Number 1" beneath which he wrote a description of the piece of fieldstone. That night, he decided, he would draw a sketch of it and record its weight and measurements.

On his way home, he bought a small box of coloured pencils.

He dug more slowly that evening, realising that it was important to record where things were found, Watching *Horizon* had left its mark, however, he knew he wouldn't ever get to the brush and trowel stage, nor would he stake out a grid at the bottom of the pit. That was too slow, and after ten thousand years, nothing would be exactly where it should be anyway. No, the important thing was to get the objects themselves.

Even though his pace of work was slower, he still dug and sifted seven barrow loads.

The Pit

He was particularly careful in looking at the stones in the sluice-box, but he found nothing.

It was dark when he went inside and began to draw the stone. Though no artist, his rendering was accurate and recognisable. He weighed it on the kitchen scales (14oz.) and measured it, using the metric side of his ruler, knowing that that was how archaeologists did it.

When he had finished, he speculated on the people who had marked it; what they had marked it for, and why.

He came to think of the men who had worked it as "the Pit People." How sad to think that this crude stone was all that was left behind.

During the following week, Norman Dodge's excitement grew. He had turned up three more stones which the Pit People had worked. One looked very much like an adze, but not quite; the second seemed to be a bit of broken spear-head; and the last one looked like nothing in particular, though it had two gouges in it.

Again, he measured, sketched and labelled them and placed them on the mantle.

From time to time, he would place the four of them on his desk and stare at them, trying to imagine them in use and attempting to divine something about their makers from them.

The spear-head, thought Norman Dodge, was an indication that they were hunters; the adze blade could

Undivulged Crimes

have been used for most anything: cutting vegetation, trimming hides, or slaughter. The stones with the grooves were more difficult to guess at. The grooves were made differently on each one, but they could have been used as weights or counters, he thought. There was really no way of knowing without finding more evidence.

The indications, Norman Dodge thought, were that the Pit People were fairly clever, maybe not advanced, but nonetheless clever. It was enough to make him very pleased that he had begun to dig and that he had persevered through those weeks of finding nothing but dirt.

Norman Dodge made another decision that night. He decided that the time for some rudimentary research had come. Now that he knew of the existence of the Pit People, he would try to find if anything had been written about them.

After work the next day, he went to the library and read through several books on pre-historic Britain. It seemed that tribes had lived all over the place, except in his area of Oxfordshire.

But it was the perfect site for them, he thought: good farming land, probably safely wooded, and the stream! He searched several volumes about the early history of the region until the library closed.

For the next week, the pit lay idle, as Norman Dodge ploughed through the library. He had learned how to use

The Pit

the card and periodical indices and was now seized by a new obsession: he had to get into the Bodlean.

For someone with no university connections, that is no simple task. The very thought of it is intimidating. His co-workers at Cowley were not in a position to use their influence, either.

However, like other problems, this one too found a solution when Norman Dodge happened upon a notice in a bookshop (he had taken to visiting book shops) announcing a meeting of a local historical society.

He attended the meeting in a gloomy church hall and listened to a lecture about the entertaining habits of seventeenth century college principals. It was excruciatingly dull, and he nearly decided to slip out quietly. Eventually, it ended, and there were few questions. He was somewhat relieved to realise that he was not the only person who had failed to find the talk stimulating, though everyone was most polite.

Coffee and biscuits were served, and it was while he was waiting for a mug that the chairman of the society approached him.

"This is your first meeting, is it not?"

"Yes," Dodge answered.

He was about to apologise for his presumption of the refreshment, but the chairman cut him off.

Undivulged Crimes

"Splendid. We're always glad to see new faces. Let me give you an application form. Did you enjoy tonight's talk?"

Dodge mumbled, but the chairman understood.

"Not you're period, eh? Nor mine either. Mine is the second fortnight in October of 1843."

"I - I - "

"That's a little joke of mine. Historians today are always accused of being too narrow in their view. Peddigrew. Northcott Peddigrew," he offered his hand.

Dodge put down his mug and Jaffa cake, and extended his hand, but by then Peddigrew had a mug of coffee in his.

"Norman Dodge."

"And what's your period, Dr Dodge?"

"I'm hardly a specialist," Dodge said. "Though I have, of late, developed an interest in pre-historic Oxfordshire."

"But there was no Oxfordshire in pre-history!" Peddigrew exclaimed.

"I beg your pardon?"

"Oh, I am sorry. Another of my little jokes. Oxfordshire didn't properly come into being until Roman times. But do go on. Do you live near a pre- historic site?"

"I live in Little Mittering."

Dodge thought this might provoke an out-pouring of the village's history.

The Pit

"I don't know of anything there, except the delightful little mediaeval stream, I fancy you know it."

"As a matter of fact, it passes through my land. Mediaeval, you say?"

How easy it was to affect the academic banter.

"Yes. Dug to supply the old priory when their well dried up or went bad. Runs for nearly ten miles. Most impressive."

"Peddigrew, where would I find the best books on the prehistory of the area?"

"The Bodlean, of course."

"But I can't get in."

"A minor problem, Dodge. Fill in your application – with the appropriate fee, of course – and I'll write you a letter saying you are a member in good standing undertaking *bona fide* research. There will be no problem. And you might want to meet Mr Ridley. He's an enthusiast of the Druids. Might be able to help you. He's over there, let me introduce you."

Ridley was very nearly a carbon copy of Peddigrew, though his interests were not confined to a fortnight in 1843.

Ridley, though not domineering, expressed with some confidence that there had been no stone, bronze, Druidical or other pre-historical habitation of the area around Little Mittering.

Undivulged Crimes

"It would have been dense forest, and with no water, it would have been a most undesirable spot for dwelling," Ridley said. "You ought to visit the Museum of Mankind and see their collection of stone age implements, if you haven't already."

Damn experts, thought Norman Dodge on the way home. Though admission to the Bodlean was virtually assured, which was all that he wanted in the first place.

At home, he handled the sacred objects of the Pit People. They were possessed of reassuring qualities. Their weights and shapes were pleasing. If no one believed in the Pit People, it didn't matter – in fact, it was all to the good: his would be the claim of discovery, and his alone.

He resumed digging on the weekend and made what he considered to be his most spectacular find: a rounded stone with human features.

Very crude, to be sure; but rough hollows for the eyes and a gouge approximately where a mouth should be. Norman Dodge scrubbed it thoroughly and examined it under his magnifying glass. Though there were no tool marks, there wouldn't necessarily be any after all that time, would there? This couldn't be a geological accident, could it? Well, maybe on its own it could, but not in the context of the other findings. Surely not.

He sketched it, weighed it, measured it, labelled it and put it on the mantle with the others.

The Pit

A week later, letter in hand, he presented himself at the Bodlean. They read the letter, made him fill out forms, took his picture, gave him his card and a booklet explaining the rules of the library and its layout and turned him loose.

A man of true intellectual curiosity would have spent several hours browsing at random and wandering through the scholarly labyrinth, but accounting had so disciplined Norman Dodge that he headed straight for the catalogues and began listing the works he wished to peruse.

He called up half a dozen and searched their indices, scanned their maps and read the relevant sections. He sacrificed a full week's digging to page through one dusty book after another when his hands longed for the feel of the damp earth and rough stones.

While he acquired an extensive knowledge of the movements of pre-historic men around Oxfordshire, none ever seemed to have gone near Little Mittering. An uninteresting place throughout time, he thought.

He spent much time studying pictures of known artefacts, and had to admit that they didn't look much like any he had found.

But why should they? The Pit People were different. Unknown, and unlike any tribe so far discovered. There was only one thing for it: collect all the evidence and write it up. He could begin by speaking to the local

Undivulged Crimes

history society. He wrote Peddigrew thanking him for the letter of introduction, and promised to see him at next month's meeting. Though tempted to say something of his discoveries, he restrained himself, knowing that a premature disclosure could have all sorts of undesirable ramifications.

He returned to digging. He was now at a depth of fourteen feet and the ramps were becoming steep. Soon he would have to increase the grade even more to get him down to twenty feet.

There was a more worrying problem facing him, too. From time to time, water would collect at the bottom of the pit. It made work difficult, and the lowest ramp was soft and sometimes muddy. He thought it was probably seepage from the stream, for he was now down to that level.

The wet earth was heavy and his barrow loads had to be smaller. He turned up another rock, shaped rather like a bone with thick ends tapering to a leaner middle. He could think of no obvious use for it and had seen nothing like it in any of the books. A pestle, perhaps? But to grind what? The ends were rough, so it didn't look like it had been used as a grinding tool.

Nevertheless, it found its way into the notebook and onto the mantel piece.

The Pit

The Pit People, Norman Dodge thought. Living away from water. A reclusive tribe. Why? By design or because they were outcasts?

Perhaps they were the magic makers. Since there were few signs of – well, there were few signs of anything – but suppose, just suppose, they were special. Non-labouring magic men. Food offerings and water would be brought to them: distant forerunners of the Druid priests. Mystics living in a sacred grove. Their power kept them apart. Honouring them would ensure good hunting, crops or whatever.

It didn't seem very likely to Norman Dodge, but then again, stranger things were done by primitive cultures. Nothing like these Pit People had ever been found, he knew that now for a fact. And somehow it seemed logical: the belief in unknown forces influenced by a special breed. Sun, rain, earth and moon gods.

He examined his most recent find again. Holding it in its tapered middle, it did not feel unlike a sceptre, some antique symbol of authority.

The grooved stones now took on the notion of real mathematical instruments, used, perhaps to measure or even predict the seasons.

The feeling grew within Norman Dodge that these Pit People were no ordinary breed. Nothing they had was recognisable because they didn't do recognisable things.

Undivulged Crimes

And the objects which the Pit People had would not be possessed by mere common folk.

It all fit.

He couldn't go on thinking of them as the "Pit People" since they plainly didn't dwell in a pit. "Grove Dwellers" or "Woodlanders" was nearer the mark, but he had for so long thought of them as the Pit People, he couldn't stop, though he would not call them that in his monograph.

The evenings were growing noticeably shorter. Combined with the weight of the wet earth and the steepness of the ramps, work progressed considerably more slowly.

By the time the next historical society meeting came round, Norman Dodge had dug to eighteen feet. Water was increasingly a problem, but he had his eye out for an old hand pump that, attached to a hose with a strainer on the end, would solve that problem.

At the meeting ("The Development of Bridge Building in Oxfordshire") Norman Dodge thanked Peddigrew and Ridley for their assistance.

"Tell me, Dodge," Ridley began, "your interest in prehistoric Oxfordshire: does this stem from some chance discovery you might have made?"

Before Norman Dodge could answer, Peddigrew interrupted.

"Ridley, I shall never understand your leaps of logic. Not at all the thing for an historian."

The Pit

"Quite logical, really, Peddigrew. Dr Dodge here has had, by his own admission, no academic training and about as much prior interest in history or archeology as – as an accountant, for example – forgive me, Dr Dodge. Yet, suddenly he acquires a passion for the stone age. He is known to have land in Little Mittering and has specifically asked about the area. Now, most people begin with a fascination for old railway lines, bridges, or some such thing, then work their way back to the mediaeval period – using the university buildings for practising their observations. But not our Dr Dodge."

Norman Dodge wished members of the society wouldn't call him doctor.

"I suppose I follow that," said Peddigrew. "But tell me, Ridley, would I be correct in inferring from what you have just said that you are an *aficionado* of detective mysteries?"

Ridley turned bright red and retired in search of another Jaffa cake.

"You must tell me if Ridley is correct in his wild guessing," Peddigrew said.

Norman Dodge consider this for a moment.

"Yes," he said finally. "Yes, I believe you could say that Ridley is largely correct."

"You have been excavating?"

"Deeply."

Undivulged Crimes

"I should very much like to visit your site," Peddigrew said with enthusiasm. "Have you unearthed anything interesting?"

"Not many things, but some. You understand that I wish to remain discreet about it until my work is complete."

"Yes, of course. But I hope that doesn't preclude a visit."

Again, Norman Dodge hesitated. Genuine academic advice would have to be sought eventually. Better it come from an acquaintance.

"Not at all. I'm usually back at the farm by five-thirty, and weekends are devoted to digging."

"Excellent!" said Peddigrew.

Norman Dodge was pleased with Peddigrew's interest.

The story of the Pit People would soon be known and the academic heavy-weights would refine what he had done. The spade-work was nearly over, literally and figuratively.

On Monday and Tuesday, Norman Dodge continued his digging. The myths of the Pit People formed vividly in his mind. Their reverence for trees, for pine needles and their joy in the sounds of wild animals. While the rest of the pre-historic tribes cast their eyes to the stars, the Pit People, unable to see the stars through the trees,

The Pit

concentrated on the earth: the sun, the wind and the rain.

As if to suggest the correctness of his suppositions, it rained on Wednesday. A long, hard, penetrating rain. It prevented Norman Dodge from working, but it gave him time to reconsider his objects and his ideas.

They pleased him.

On Thursday, he hoped that Peddigrew would not come. The pit was muddy and looked merely like a hole in the ground as might be made for a new office block, though a deal untidier.

He set about cleaning it up. Nearly a foot of water had collected in the bottom, and bailing was not an easy operation: a wheel barrow full of water not being the easiest thing to manoeuvre up a muddy slope.

He loaded about ten gallons into the metal barrow and had begun to push it up the first ramp when he was taken by a curious sensation. There seemed to be motion all round him, but when he looked around, everything seemed normal.

He lifted the barrow handles and pushed forward before he noticed himself sinking.

The ramp was giving way and he stood still and felt the spongy, sickly feeling of the sinking ramp.

The wheel barrow tipped and dumped its load of water back into the pit and soon Norman Dodge felt himself falling after it.

Undivulged Crimes

☙

"Rather a mess, isn't it, Peddigrew?" Ridley asked. They looked into the pit at the over-turned wheel barrow and the drowned body of Norman Dodge.

"Yes. These amateurs always make a mess," Peddigrew said with disdain. "Doesn't look like there was much there, does it?"

Ridley shrugged.

"Pity we have to call the police. If only we could just fill it in," he mused. "Ha! That would be a puzzle for someone in five thousand years or so!"

"Pity."

Ridley and Peddigrew went to the house to ring the constabulary.

While Ridley was on the phone, Peddigrew nosed around. He found the objects on the mantle and the notebook on the desk.

"The police will be here in twenty minutes," Ridley said. "What have you got there?"

"Dodge's notes."

"Anything interesting?"

"No, just curious. Fairly methodical in his own way. Look at these sketches."

"They're not bad."

"What are they?"

"Just odd rocks."

"You mean they're not real?"

The Pit

"Real rocks, Ridley."

Ridley looked at the collection. "Not an artefact among 'em."

The two men sat silently waiting for the police.

"Peddigrew?" Ridley said after a few minutes.

"Hmmm?"

"There could be some fun in this, you know."

"Fun?"

"Mmm. There are bound to be stories in the papers: 'Eccentric Archeologist Drowns in Pit.' That sort of thing."

"Go on, Ridley," said Peddigrew with growing enthusiasm.

"It would be a great opportunity for an academic follow-up: 'Amateur's Discovery: The Legend of the Little Mittering Pit People;' something like that."

Peddigrew mused for a moment.

"You might be onto something. You know, the idea rather appeals to me."

"It would certainly break the academic tedium."

"Indeed."

Undivulged Crimes

Winter Wind

Winter Wind

Undivulged Crimes

Winter Wind

Russian stories of the 19th century are problematic for modern readers, not because of the complexity of plot, or foreignness of custom or psychology, but because of the ritualistic nature of the characters' names.

For those not familiar with the convention, Russian Christian names are like those in the West: family names, saints' names (often from the feast celebrated on the child's birthday), or simply names parents can agree on.

These names are familiar – or nearly – to us: Alexander, Nicholas, Gregory, Peter; Anna, Sofia. Nadezhda, is seldom heard today in Russia, and virtually never in the West.

The diminutives of these names are used by friends and family: Alexi, Nicky, Anya, Nadya.

To distinguish the many Alexis and Anyas, a middle name, constructed from the father's name, is added. In our story, it is Alexandr Nikolovitch and Anya Dimitrinovna.

The use of nicknames that may or may not be related to the Christian name, Sasha for Alexandr or Alexandra, Natasha or Tasha for Natalya, have been avoided in this story.

On arrival at the Karpovs' house, the formality – which would have begun the evening and then relaxed – is revived until the party has settled in, and the evening is once again a party of old friends. Only the young Count Peter and his wife, the Countess Nadya Ivanovna maintain the formality, either from deference to age, or youthful insecurity.

Undivulged Crimes

Personal preference may also be inferred to play a role. Prince Grigor, for example, is only twice referred to with his middle name. There is obviously something in his character or preference that enables the familiarity.

Characters

Prince Alexandr Grigorovitch Karpov, Alexi, host of the opera party, a captain in the Imperial Russian Navy

General Nickolai Karpov, his father, retired from the army, and with his son, wealthy land-owners

Prince Gregor Igorovitch, an old friend of the general's and a retired general himself

Princess Sofia Alexandrovna, his wife, who too much likes cake

Count Peter Kutzov, a young army officer, the son of friends of both generals, uneasy in such august company, and eager not to offend

Countess Nadya Ivanovna, married to Count Peter, and equally insecure, for no reason

Duchess Anya Dimitrinovna, possibly the most eligible heiress in all the Russias; fiancé Kiril, killed while serving in the army; assumed future wife of Prince Alexi

Winter Wind

11 Ноябрь 1901

It was after eleven when the party arrived at Prince Alexi's. Laughing while pulling coats, furs and long scarves about them amid swirling snow, they climbed down from the carriages to the line of footmen who offered arms, held open doors, and bowed their heads. Snowflakes landed on their powdered wigs and vanished, but stood out on the shoulders and sleeves of their blue coats.

Flambeaux burned on either side of the arched doorway, and shadows flickered on the walls and fresh snow. Gusts of wind blew eddies of snow and nearly dislodged a young servant's wig as he led Princess Sofia to the steps. Her husband, Prince Grigor followed, steadied by Count Peter Kutzov. The Duchess Nadya, Count Peter's wife, followed with another footman. Lastly Prince Alexi led the Duchess Anya Dmitrinovna Rashnokova.

"We are as scattered as the snow," said the Duchess Anya. "Peter isn't looking after his wife, nor Nadya Ivanovna after her husband."

"It makes it difficult for the servants," Prince Alexi observed with a chuckle. "They don't know whom to attend."

Undivulged Crimes

"It's very bad manners," said the duchess. "Just because we are all friends is no reason to neglect our customs."

"My dear Anya," said the Prince Alexi. "You are far too young to worry about the decline of manners."

The duchess did not reply, but looked up at the great house. Light shone from its windows on two floors and white smoke rose from a dozen chimneys. She looked up until the snowflakes on her eyelashes made her look down, and she wiped them away.

"Good evening, Duchess," said the Prince's *majordomo*, when they had mounted the steps and arrived at the door.

"Thank you, Kornenko," she replied with a small smile.

The door was shut behind them and the noise of the wind shut out.

The party had passed into the large foyer, lit with dozens of candles and the fire, around which they gathered.

Hats and coats were removed and carried away, while a servant passed among them offering champagne.

"An end to a splendid evening," said Prince Grigor, raising his glass, first to his wife and then to Prince Alexi.

Prince Grigor had been a friend of Prince Alexi's father, General Nikolai. Now well into his seventies, he yet retained his military bearing, trim figure and economy

Winter Wind

with words. He had silver hair, and a full growth of beard on his cheeks, cut in the style the English called "mutton chops."

His wife, the Princess Sofia, was enjoying, late in life, the attentions of a husband who had been away for many of their younger years, but his affection had not diminished. A small woman, she had eaten her way to contentment in her husband's absence. He seemed neither to have noticed nor cared, and remained devoted to her.

They toasted and laughed for a few moments before Prince Alexi placed his empty flute on a silver tray and said, "Shall we proceed to supper?"

Amid expressions of consent, the prince raised his arm slightly, and Duchess Anya immediately placed her gloved hand on it. They exchanged a gentle smile and watched as the guests moved up the stairs with its rich blue carpet and elegantly carved details. It was elegant, not ornate. The beauty of the Karpov house lay not in opulence, but in its well-crafted, and judiciously executed detail. The strength of the building was in its adherence to classical proportion. Rooms, doors, windows, and views from one room to the next had been carefully planned. So well had the house been conceived that apart from the occasional redecoration, and various modernisations of the kitchens, plumbing and heating arrangements, the house had not changed in nearly a hundred years.

There had been periods when it was thought to be too austere; there would no doubt be a time when it was considered too detailed, yet for those who had lived in it, both masters and servants, it had been a comfortable home.

Despite its size, it had a welcoming warmth that Prince Alexi recognised each time he returned from an expedition. He intended to live the rest of his life here, though who would succeed him in its occupancy was uncertain.

Prince Alexi and the duchess moved up the stairs easily, exchanging a light remark about the good spirits of the guests, and their appetites for the awaiting supper.

The sounds of laughter and hearty greetings could be heard from the salon as Prince Grigor encountered his old friend the general.

"Nikolai, you are looking splendid!" Prince Grigor exclaimed.

The general was standing, and reached out to take the hand of Princess Sofia, and bowed to kiss it. Prince Alexi's father was nearly eighty and retained as much of his dignity as the years that had passed would allow. Though now portly and prone to illness – especially in consequence of the cold – General Nikolai retained his

Winter Wind

perception, wit and love of history, though he endeavoured not to bore people.

Count Peter and the Duchess Nadya followed, paying their respects to Prince Alexi's father.

"And how was the opera?" the general inquired.

"There were three!" Duchess Nadya said enthusiastically. "Two by Cui, and Rimsky-Korsakov's *Mozart and Salieri*."

"Indeed, the general said. "Did you speak to the great Cesar afterwards to praise his success?"

"No, we did not," said Duchess Nadya, as though admitting to a grave omission. "But the operas were very pleasant."

Prince Grigor came to the young duchess's rescue.

"Don't mind what Nikolai says, my dear. We both knew Cui in the army. He designed many of the fortifications we occupied over the years, and he builds operas just as well."

"It is a pity you missed it, Prince Nikolai," said the duchess Anya, stepping forward to greet him.

He did not kiss her hand, but embraced her, kissing both her cheeks. He then repeated the affectionate gesture to his son.

"Alas, I would have liked to have gone," the general replied, "but I am so nearly over my cough that I didn't wish to risk its return, and my doctor forbade it. He said

Undivulged Crimes

it would not do to have someone coughing through an opera about the plague."

He laughed easily with his son and these friends.

Prince Grigor he had known since his entrance to the army. The prince had just completed his training and Prince Nikolai was still a captain. Prince Nikolai had begun as a mentor, but they soon became friends. When Prince Grigor married Sofia Alexandrovna Malikov, the sister of an old school friend, their friendship was sealed for life.

"I know you enjoy opera," said Princess Sofia, "and there would have been nothing tonight that you wouldn't have found delightful. You would have recognised two of the arias from *Feast in Time of Plague*, as they have been performed before."

"I have heard *Mozart and Salieri* before, and have read the stories," said the general. "Both Cui and Rimsky-Korsakov are always good to listen to, unlike Tchaikovski who never knows when to shut up. And how was Chalyapin?"

"What a voice!" exclaimed Duchess Nadya, who heard the question. "I had not heard him before but I shall go to hear him again."

The Duchess Nadya was very young, slight and insecure. Her husband, Count Peter, almost equally young, and clearly adored his pretty wife, but shared her

Winter Wind

youthful lack of confidence in such company. As such, he was unable to support her with mature assurance.

Prince Alexi noted that the servants had opened the doors to the dining room. Places had not been set, but a buffet arranged on the table, and several piles of small plates and an array of cutlery indicated that many returns for different dishes would be made.

"This is splendid!" said Prince Grigor, advancing.

The Duchess Anya had moved to join Duchess Nadya and Count Peter, sensing that being the youngest at the party by a considerable number of years, knew that they might feel awkward.

"Did you organise this evening's party?" Count Peter asked Duchess Anya. "It's not the sort of thing Prince Alexi does unprompted. Though he always seems to enjoy himself."

The duchess smiled.

"Alexi does enjoy music. Unknown to most people, he's a fine pianist," said the duchess. "As to parties, he enjoys the small affairs like this, or a dozen for dinner more than large parties."

Duchess Nadya laughed.

"You are very clever, Anya Dmitrinovna," she said, adding, when she saw that neither the duchess nor her husband understood what she meant, "You haven't answered the question at all!"

Duchess Anya laughed quietly.

Undivulged Crimes

"Yes, I confess to having had a hand in it," she said. "Alexi hasn't entertained for a while, and the general was in need of some diversion, even if he couldn't go to the performance. Dear Peter, you would not mind very much if your wife flirted with the general for a while this evening?"

They all laughed.

"I have no objection at all," said the count, "as long as you keep me entertained while she does."

"Peter!" his wife exclaimed. "You must not embarrass Duchess Anya!"

"I am not embarrassed, Nadya," the duchess replied. "It is a fair request if I am to deprive him of your company. During dessert, perhaps?"

The count bowed to Anya and she moved to speak to Princess Sofia, who was returning to the salon with a plate of food, followed by a servant carrying her wine glass. Count Peter and his wife watched as Duchess Anya helped the old princess to her chair and then engage her in easy conversation.

"Why has that delightful lady never married?" Count Peter asked his wife.

The young duchess looked wistfully at the departing figure of Anya Dmitrinovna.

"She was engaged once," Nadya Ivanovna said *sotto voce* to her husband. "He was killed in one of our army's glorious campaigns. Anya Dmitrinovna wasn't yet

Winter Wind

twenty, and took it very badly. She lived with her parents until such a time that she had to remain longer and look after them. And now, she's alone, with a very nice apartment in Moscow, a grander one in St Petersburg, and estates in the country."

"She is not with Prince Alexi because she needs money, then?" Count Peter asked.

"Not at all," his wife answered.

Countess Nadya was about to continue but they became suddenly aware of someone standing near them. Turning they saw it was Princess Sofia, on her way to fetch some more food. She gave them a kindly smile.

"I could not bear to take more food before you had anything to eat," she said with a sense of self-parody. "But I could not help but hear you were speculating about the lovely, lonely, duchess. She is truly kind, and one hopes that things will work out for her in the end."

Neither the count nor his wife spoke, mostly from embarrassment, but Princess Sofia took it as a cue to continue.

"Don't worry about talking about Anya Dmitrinovna," she said. "All of Moscow and St Petersburg are making the same speculation. It would be a good solution, though. The prince is heirless, and she is alone and full of love. Each has more money and property than would be needed by the next three generations. The only question is, are they brave enough?"

Undivulged Crimes

"You have known the duchess long?" Count Peter asked.

"Since she was a little girl," Sofia Alexandrovna replied. "I was an acquaintance of her mother. "We could have been very close friends, but most of the year she lived very far away. We'd see each other at the theatre and at balls during the winter season, and sometimes we'd be at the same parties, but Tatiana knew it was for a short time, and never confided in me – or anyone else in Moscow that I knew.

"After Tatiana Petronovna married, she came to Moscow more often and used to take Anya Dmitrinovna around to visit. She was a nice, unpretentious girl, which was a rare thing."

Duchess Nadya was fascinated with the old princess's story.

"I'll tell you a little more if you come with me into the dining room," she said, her eyes twinkling as she remembered younger days.

The count and the countess took plates from the pile and selected their food. The old princess gave hers to a servant and waved to a small table by the wall with several chairs and a candle stick on it. The servant put the princess's food, and a new glass of wine, on the table, and went to fetch a light for the candle.

When the trio had seated, and taken a few mouthfuls, Sofia Alexandrovna resumed. "It was hardly surprising

Winter Wind

that Anya Dmitrinovna would find a clever and handsome young man to fall in love with. I never met him, nor knew his family, but his name, I think, was Kiril. He was well-educated and prepared for a career in the army.

"It was a bad time," she said reflecting. "Our dear Alexander, who had done so much for us was murdered." The old princess blessed herself in remembrance of the dead czar, and the young duchess felt an impulse to do the same.

"Alexander Alexandrovitch became our czar and the troubles increased. Kiril, as a young officer, was quickly in the middle of things – within weeks of the announcement of their engagement. I was invited to that party, but was suffering from influenza.

"Kiril, they say, was a reasonable man in unreasonable times. If you ever wondered why Prince Alexi was in the navy instead of the army with the general, that is why. By the time he was ready to serve the tsar and Mother Russia, there were other grave problems, and old Prince Nikolai placed young Alexi Nikolaivitch in the navy where he'd be safer."

Count Peter looked shocked and opened his mouth to express his sense of anger, disappointment, outrage.

"Do not condemn Prince Nikolai, or Prince Alexi. They have done nothing shameful or cowardly. Both have served the tsar well and risked their lives for our safety. They also acted judiciously, and prudently," said

Undivulged Crimes

Princess Sofia. "Young people see things more absolutely. Do you think that Prince Alexi did not want to follow his father into the army? Had he not dreamt of it all his life? When you have children of your own, you will see how your attitude modifies."

They sat silently for a few moments and ate. The servant filled their glasses and moved away.

"What did Anya Dmitrinova do once her fiancé died?" asked Nadya Ivanovna.

"She returned to the country, and after her parents died, she took over running the estates. She managed them actively, like Prince Alexi does. Their knowledge of agriculture is comprehensive."

"It is said that their combined estates would be one percent of Russia," said Count Peter.

"Lots of things are said," the old princess replied waving her hand.

"It is also said that they will marry," said Nadya Ivanovna.

"Indeed, it is; and I hope they do, for both deserve the security."

"Not happiness?" the young duchess asked.

"One must not ask for too much," Princess Sofia replied with a laugh. "Security is valuable, and can protect one from the winds of change."

Winter Wind

She stood and smiled kindly at the count and his wife and walked to the salon to join the others, followed by the servant with her wine glass.

The count finished his drink and laughed.

"Well my darling Natasha, has that given you enough to think about?" he asked. "In that little narrative, you had the whole of Russian history: love, war, disappointment, and murder."

The young duchess looked at him wide-eyed, then bowed her head and sobbed.

"Why am I so consumed with pettiness and miss the realities of life?" she asked, looking up at her husband with a face full of tears. "How can you love someone so shallow?"

The count stood and held his hand out to her. Still looking miserable, she shook her head and turned slightly from him.

"No one shallow would think such a thing," Count Peter said, continuing to hold out his hand. "Nadya Ivanovna?"

Seeing his steadfastness, she took his hand and he helped her to stand. She looked up at him, her face full of questions. He took his handkerchief and gently dabbed her face and eyes. Nadya Ivanovna gave him a small, resolute smile and they walked into the salon.

৪০

Undivulged Crimes

"My dear Peter," said Prince Alexi to him as he came through the archway to the salon.

At the same moment, the Duchess Anya Dmitrinovna greeted Nadya Ivanovna and led her to a sofa near the fire. It was a more comfortable place to sit than it looked with its yellow watered silk and carved wooden ornamentation. Several small pillows were propped in the corners, which Duchess Anya rearranged to suit her before she sat down.

"Did you get enough to eat, Nadya Ivanovna?" she asked. "And did you have a nice chat with Princess Sofia?"

The young countess looked at her hands. Sensing the awkwardness, Duchess Anya continued, "I always find Princess Sofia such good company. She is very modern in her attitudes and can be very amusing. Most of all, she is kind."

Nadya Ivanovna nodded and looked up.

"Yes, she is very kind."

"What did you talk about? Did you have a good gossip?"

Nadya Ivavnovna started to look down again, but stopped herself.

"We were speaking of the operas," she answered.

"And did you enjoy them?"

"Very much," Nadya Ivanovna said smiling briefly. "*The Mandarin's Son* made me laugh very much. Do you enjoy opera?"

Winter Wind

The Duchess Anya smiled at this easy turning of the question back on herself, but didn't protest.

"I spent much of my life in the country and we had to make our own music, but when I was in Moscow or St Petersburg, I was always eager to go to concerts, the theatre and the opera.

"You made your own music?" Countess Nadya asked.

"My father played the cello, and sometimes the violin. Mother and I played the piano, either to accompany him or to play duets. We'd have all sorts of music sent to us."

"I expect you were a wonderful player – do you still play?"

"Indeed, she does," said Prince Alexi, who had approached during their conversation. "I was just about to ask the dear duchess to play for us now,"

"Please, Alexi," she replied modestly. "After an evening of wonderful music, it's not right that I play."

Prince Alexi smiled at Nadya Ivanovna, then at Duchess Anya.

"I did not come to insist," he said, "merely to suggest that Father, and the others might enjoy some music. One piece, perhaps?"

Nadya Ivanovna was fascinated by the exchange that was playing out before her. Was Duchess Anya to be commanded by Prince Alexi? But that was no command, but a polite suggestion. Did she feel she must comply? Or, was this an opportunity for her to exert a measure of

Undivulged Crimes

independence? There wasn't the hint of a barb in their conversation. How she wished she understood the relationship between these two people.

Nadya Ivanovna knew they were very old, close friends who had, in their time, shared dreams, secrets, fears, disappointments, and argued, too. For all that, here they were, still in each other's company and much of society expected them to marry.

Emerging from her reflection, she became aware that Prince Alexi with impeccable military strategy had prepared the campaign before engaging the duchess, The others had arranged themselves to face the piano, and the general was even now raising the lid.

Then Anya Dmitrinovna stood.

"Forgive me, Nadya Ivanovna. I am commanded to perform."

Nadya Ivanovna nodded, but was well aware of the irony that was intended. Indeed, she was smiling as she was escorted to the keyboard, and Prince Alexi held the chair for her.

The duchess closed her eyes for a moment before precisely striking the quiet, but foreboding notes of Chopin's Etude Op. 25, Number 11. Everyone in the room knew it, and as she reached the warm gentle chords, awaited the turbulence that followed.

The duchess played flawlessly, and drove the piece with the relentless force of Chopin's intention. Halfway through the piece where the fortissimo chords are followed by momentary silences before the storm begins anew, the silence in the salon was palpable, and more stunning still was the concentration of Anya Dmitrinovna. She retained her force, for a dozen seconds after the rapid rising sequence at the end of the piece, and her audience, too, remained silent until she relaxed and stood up.

The men clapped while Princess Sofia and Duchess Nadya expressed pleasure and amazement at her performance. Prince Alexi went to the duchess and kissed her cheeks, then took her hand and raised it in triumph to the others. The duchess lowered her head and smiling gave a little bob before joining the general and Princess Sofia.

"A most appropriate piece," said Princess Sofia. "And wonderfully played."

"Thank you, Sofia Alexandrovna, but I suspect you are the only one to grasp my meaning."

"I wish you would play more," said the general, "but I can see that it was very strenuous and the hour is late."

Not far away, Prince Grigor had engaged Prince Alexi, who had been moving to speak with Count Peter.

"You know of course, Alexi Nikolaivitch, that all Moscow and St Petersburg are hoping you will marry that kind and dear lady, and have been so hoping for many years."

Undivulged Crimes

"If only I were worthy of her, our house would be honoured and renewed," Prince Alexi replied. "But what can I offer? I am away much of the time and suspect the world is becoming more dangerous."

"Dear boy!" exclaimed Prince Grigor. "Give yourself a little more than that! You could give her a future that wasn't lonely, and perhaps children to continue both your lines. Oh, Anya Dmitronovna has a considerable fortune – and by all accounts manages her estates admirably – but a great fortune and vast areas of land are not a great comfort as one grows older. Think on it Alexi Nikolaivitch."

The prince nodded to the old family friend, who had always, and even now, acted as an uncle to him.

"Do you think this is not in my mind?" Prince Alexi asked. "Anya Dimtrinovnva is, as you say, a remarkable, kind and clever woman. More clever than I, and though not a musician myself, in her music I can see and hear such depths of awareness, passion and insight that I know I am no match for her, and believe me, it makes me grieve.

"So, I go back to my ships and live in a world that I know and can cope with."

The old prince looked saddened, but his eyes still twinkled.

"Sometimes all a woman like that really wants is someone to take her in his arms and say 'I love you',"

Prince Grigor said, and then turned to the Duchess Nadya who was passing, while Prince Alexi resumed his progress to Count Peter.

The count turned to him as he approached.

"Prince Alexi," said the count differentially. "Nadya Ivanovna and I are honoured to be included in this intimate party."

"It is our pleasure, Peter Petrovitch," the prince answered. "When Anya Dmitrinovna told me of your wife's love of music, I knew you would enjoy speaking to Grigor Igorovitch and Father. With dedicated military men, I knew it would be a fine evening."

"Your father is still very much up to date in military matters," said Count Peter.

"He is, and he is very glad of someone to speak about the army with, since he cannot do it with me. I am sure he would be grateful of your company should you care to pass an afternoon with an old man."

"If you are serious, Prince Alexi, it would be an honour. The general, as you must know well, is held in very high esteem, even though it is twenty years since he held a command. I know he is a regular advisor to the government at the highest levels."

"You do not need to flatter me or my father, Peter Petrovitch. In this house, honesty is enough," said Prince Alexi.

Undivulged Crimes

"Yet it is true, Alexi Nikolaivitch. Prince Nikolai has the respect and affection of officers and men alike."

"It is a pity I cannot claim the same admiration myself," Prince Alexi said.

Count Peter fell silent, and Prince Alexi, noting his embarrassment, spoke.

"Do not worry yourself, my friend," laughed the prince. "It is our nature to take things too seriously, but I fear there is great unrest in the world and the Russias will not escape these winds of change."

"From where do you see this threat arising, Prince Alexi?" Count Peter asked, clearly troubled by the prince's thoughts.

"From within ourselves," he replied quietly. "We have moved into an age of mechanisation. We have moved from sail to steam in a generation and will move to oil, gas or electricity in the next. Vehicles with engines will make our wars, and weapons of equal ingenuity."

"Surely these things will enable wars to be settled sooner."

"But at what cost?" the prince replied. "The field of battle will enlarge itself to take in towns and cities in a way that has never been possible before. A modern Napoleon could flatten Moscow before entering what was left. No one in the civilian population would be safe."

"I hope you do not brood too much on these things, Alexi Nikolaivitch," said the count. "For while they may

Winter Wind

be true, it is part of our job to see that it does not come to pass."

Prince Alexi smiled at his young friend.

"It is, Peter Petrovitch."

Prince Alexi left the count to speak to Princess Sofia who had been speaking with the general.

"Come sit by an old lady," she said when he had greeted her.

"Only if you promise not to tell me to marry Anya Dmitrinovna," he said smiling at her.

"Then there is nothing to talk about," she reposted.

"I have already had it from Grigor Igorovitch, and indirectly from my father again."

"And what of the duchess herself?" asked the old princess.

"We have never discussed it," said the prince.

Princess Sofia laughed loudly and affected to dab her eyes.

"Why do I find that so hard to believe?" she asked.

"It is very simple," said the prince. "Everyone talks to me about it, but not one here tonight has said a word to Anya Dmitrinovna. If you are all too frightened to say anything to her, how do you think it must be for me?"

The old princess laughed easily.

"My dear Alexi Nikolaivitch. Why do you make things so complicated? Love comes from a number of things, but certainty isn't one of them. Respect, affection, dedication

Undivulged Crimes

– these are what make love take hold. You know as well as anyone that you've never considered anyone else."

"Perhaps I have known her too long," Prince Alexi said.

"What – so that there's no mystery?" Princes Sofia laughed again. "And you want certainty. *And* mystery? My dear Alexi!"

The princess shook her head and gave another laugh, and moved to a place by her husband.

Plates had been cleared away and servants brought coffee and decanters and glasses for port and brandy. As they did so, the guests came together in seats by the fire, and the number of conversations reduced.

"They say Moussorgsky sang the part of the Mandarin in the first performance," Prince Grigor was saying to the general.

"Quite true," the old man answered. "It wasn't in a theatre, though. It was in Cui's apartment! Cesar Antonovitch told me himself. It must have been a pretty ragged affair, but because it was comedy, it probably didn't matter."

There was easy laughter and divers comments about the opera, the wine, and the sudden noise of sleet hitting the windows. The curtains hadn't been drawn and the noise was as a drum roll.

"Where would Russian opera be without Pushkin?" Count Peter asked. "The German, French and the Italians get their opera plots from all over, but all ours come from Pushkin. Why not from Gorki or Chekhov? We have writers and poets from three hundred years, but it's always Pushkin."

"Do you not like Pushkin?" Princess Sofia asked.

"I have nothing against him," the young count replied, "but his influence on our operas seems out of proportion."

"It's because he has such a unifying force among us. From St Petersburg to Vladivostok, everyone knows Pushkin's tales," said Prince Grigor. "They bring us together."

"Even if they are serious conjecture," said Prince Alexi. "There is no truth in the Salieri story: it's a complete fantasy, but for a hundred years it's been put about that Salieri murdered Mozart."

"But it is such good theatre," Princess Sofia protested.

"But the arts should illuminate Truth," said Count Peter. "Art that spreads rumour or untruths isn't worthy of the name."

"This is interesting," said Prince Alexi. "So you mean that even fiction should be true? What about fantasy?"

"Or comedy," interjected the general.

"Fiction itself, by definition is not true, but it can express truths, just as can painting, music or poetry."

Undivulged Crimes

"Then why not just state the truth and be done with the fiction?" Prince Grigor asked, but his tone was curious rather than challenging.

"Because fiction is engaging," said Prince Alexi. "Few would read a book of truths, but fiction can lead the reader to the truth – or at least towards it."

"And the readers experience the sense of discovery," Count Peter continued excitedly.

"And the reader believes it all the more because he thinks it's his idea!" Prince Alexi concluded.

The prince and the count sat back in their chairs, satisfied with their digression.

"It seems a lot of effort to very little purpose," said Princess Sofia.

"But there may be little truths as well as great ones," Prince Alexi said in a conciliatory way.

"Then what is all this religious mysticism that seems to be spreading about us?" demanded the general. "Are there some truths, great or little there, or is it all *fin de siecle* nonsense?"

"It's a long way from simple faith," the Countess Nadya Ivanovnoa ventured. "Don't you think so, Prince Alexi?"

"It is not a world where I have any competence," Prince Alexi said. "But, those parts that I recognise, I do not trust."

Winter Wind

He said no more, and the room was silent in expectation.

"Pray go on," Duchess Anya Dmitrinovna said at length.

"I only mean, my dear, that the deliberate obscuring of something gives the obscurer considerable power. That that power is essentially based on nothing – that is, on the pretext that there is something that no one but the obscurer can see."

"You are becoming a very powerful man, then, my boy," said the general.

The company laughed, as did Prince Alexi, but Count Peter pursued the point.

"You are right, indeed, Alexi Nikolaivitch," said the count. "When the obvious becomes lost in a blizzard of artifice, then we are, indeed, in trouble."

"There is no doubt that these are times when we must look to our wits," replied Prince Alexi.

"We are lucky to have our senses about us," said Princess Sofia. "And we are not terrified like little children."

There were sounds of approbation from around the room. A brief silence followed this as they considered the truth of the old princess's words. Then, barely audibly, words filled the silence.

"You are all afraid."

Couples looked at one another, wondering if they had imagined the words. The general glanced at his servants

Undivulged Crimes

who remained in the room, but they were distant and impassive.

"You are all afraid," came the voice again. Then louder, "*We* are all afraid."

Heads turned and focused on the speaker.

"Anya Dmitrinovna, what can you mean?" asked Nadya Ivanovna in a small voice, full of uncertainty.

"We are all afraid," the duchess said again, now confidently. "Look at us, behind high walls, surrounded by servants and afraid to walk along the streets of Moscow."

"My dear - " the general began.

"And tonight," she continued, her voice rising, but still under full control, "we have come to a delightful supper party," she nodded to the general, "and have had easy conversation among very old friends.

"We have talked about our estates, and our friends, and acquaintances. We have spoken of military campaigns, and art, and theatre, and St Petersburg."

The duchess was now standing and speaking perfectly politely, as if at a meeting.

"We have even talked about each other and whether Prince Alexi and I, the Duchess Anya Dmitrinovna, would or should marry. But of the evening's other entertainment? Our opera party? Hardly at all."

She glanced around for a reaction, and was quite surprised by what she saw. The general looked saddened; the old princess affronted; Prince Grigor had a look of studied impassivity, a look she knew well. Count Peter looked furious, while the young countess had her eyes fixed on Anya Dmitrinovna with a frightened stare and tears streaming down her face, unnoticed by all. And Prince Alexi – Prince Alexi's look conveyed to her not only his own self-confidence, but complete, uncritical devotion.

Some reactions she could have predicted, but Nadya Ivanovna's and Alexi Nikolaivitch's she had not expected. Their expressions tempted her to yield, to apologise, and retreat to a distant bedroom, but she knew she must continue, if only so that her thoughts would become clear to herself.

"We have spoken about who was there with whom," she continued, sounding more calm. "We have spoken of Chalyapin's genius, and how we had seen *The Mandarin's Son* and *Mozart and Salieri* over the years, but of the new opera? *Feast in Time of Plague*? Not a word. A pity. It's a fine little opera. It sets off at a gallop and holds the listener with a stunning intensity all the way through, even though the pace changes and becomes lyrical until what is an inevitable end.

"Cesar Antonovitch should be well pleased tonight. The performance was excellent, and its reception enthusiastic. Everyone loves Pushkin, of course.

"But the reason you did not talk about it is the reason you are all afraid. Cesar Antonovitch has brooded over that little opera for more than twenty years. Why is that,

Undivulged Crimes

do you think? Because he, too, is afraid. But he knew he had to get it out of his system, just as I have to now, though it may cost me everything.

"Yet, it's true, and you all know it, which is why you haven't talked about it.

"Those seven people at the feast pretending not to see the reality around them aren't in ancient London or Florence. They are us. Locked in our great houses; protected and ignorant of the lives of most of our countrymen, and afraid of what may blow down the street."

The Duchess Anya Dmitrinovna gave a long sigh, and sat down.

"Like them, none of us knows what to do next."

A log in the grate shifted, but no one looked up. The servants stood passively, and the gently flickering candle flames were the only thing in the room that moved.

"I know!" Duchess Nadya exclaimed brightly. "Let's play charades!"

Angela's Wedding

Undivulged Crimes

Angela's Wedding

Angela knew there might be a problem when she announced that she intended to marry her cat.

There would be the expected fuss from the usual quarters, but this was the 21st century, and after all, she was living in California. It wasn't as though she wanted to marry a dangerous or wild animal or a close family member. Boots was just an ordinary cat.

What she hadn't expected was the explosion of outrage because Boots was a bitch.

Somehow, a "Women Against Lesbian Bestiality" group had materialized within 48 hours of the announcement being posted on LookAtMe. What Angela had thought would be a few dozen friends meeting for the ceremony and picnic in Golden Gate Park now looked like attracting a hundred thousand people. Her page was already covered with messages from city officials regarding permits, applications and fees required for policing, traffic management, parking, portable restrooms, and barriers for crowd control and management, along with indemnity policies.

Angela also received a hard lesson in online privacy, as her supposedly anonymous identity "PussyGalore-_4752" turned out not to be anonymous at all when the

Undivulged Crimes

telephone started to ring. Wedding planners, caterers, photographers, dress designers, hair stylists, make-up artists, printers, contract seating hire companies and other parasitical "service providers" seemed to circle like vultures.

She hoped this would die down quickly as all these offers of "taking away the worry" were preventing her from the business of organizing the wedding herself.

Before the calls from suppliers had stopped, the bloggers, freelancers, local newspapers and radio stations called for comments and interviews. One "proper" radio station invited Angela for an interview, but they didn't want to pay anything. There were also calls from City Hall reminding her of more regulations.

What was intended to be a simple ceremony had exploded, and if the media turned out to be against her, she felt she'd need to go into something like witness protection.

Things looked up a day later when one of the few calls she got was from LGB-TV. Surely they would stick up for her, but they were really only interested in learning why she had chosen a bitch and not a tom. Had she been gay long? What other experiences had she had, and what prejudice and discrimination had she faced?

They weren't prepared to pay, either.

She had briefly considered calling off the wedding altogether, but that would make it look like the bigots had

Angela's Wedding

won.

Later that afternoon, she got a call from an animal rights organization. She hadn't expected trouble from this quarter, either.

Was Boots consenting to this arrangement? What evidence was there? By what means had Boots given her consent?

Over the next few days, the barrage of calls, brochures and door-stopping continued.

"Could we have a picture of you with Boots?"

"When were you first attracted to cats?"

"Does she sleep on your bed, or in it?"

"Do you think you can communicate better with a cat than a man? Or a woman?"

The next phase was when the relatively mild protests evolved into denunciations and hate speech. Animal rights had not advanced enough to have animal hate-speech declared illegal.

"Animal Rights Activists Are Barking," bumper stickers appeared. They even showed up on online pop-ups which showed there was some serious money behind the campaign to thwart her happiness.

A week after her fun announcement, Angela was a virtual recluse. Her telephone was permanently off the hook; she hadn't dared check her email in four days; and, she had sealed the letter-slot in her door with a board. As she fixed it into place, a picture of the demented Vernon

Undivulged Crimes

Dursley flashed through her mind as she banged in the nails. Still, her efforts enjoyed more success than his had.

Three days after cutting herself off from the real and virtual worlds, Angela had to venture out to the supermarket for supplies. She should have realized that she would be hijacked in the pet food aisle, but was by then oblivious to the media storm that had continued to surround her forthcoming marriage.

"You're the cat lady!" an eager journalist with a microphone exclaimed, waving for her colleague with the camera who was following some tight yoga pants into the dessert section.

Angela threw some tins of chicken, fish and faux rabbit cat food into her trolley and rolled away.

"I see you have 'White Rabbit' brand faux rabbit," the journalist called. "Don't you think that's racist? And isn't Boots worth real rabbit?"

Keeping her mouth shut while waiting in the check out line, having every item in her trolley photographed and live-streamed to electronic devices worldwide, proved nearly impossible. The check-out girl showed signs of suffering from stage fright as she appeared to forget how to scan groceries and smiled vacuously at the battery of cameras and cell phones.

Taking what precautions she could to protect her debit card and PI number, Angela collected her receipt and trundled away into the car park. Ten minutes later,

Angela's Wedding

she remembered where she left her car, all the while composing the headlines that would even now be appearing.

"Racist lesbian buys future mate fake meat," was one of the kindest she came up with.

Her entourage had drifted away after heading down the third lane of parking spaces, so Angela was able to drive away uninterrupted.

Word had got out that she would be heading home, and the police had cordoned off her section of the street. She drove into her driveway and carried her shopping to the front door, only to be approached by a determined city functionary who delivered an envelope and requested a signature.

Angela had a momentary victory when she insisted he hold her shopping while she opened the front door and went in.

"Come in if you want your receipt," she called to him on the doorstep. "The shopping can go on the counter in there."

The functionary was used to following instructions (otherwise he would not have been sent to Angela's) and dutifully went into the kitchen and deposited the bags.

Angela scribbled on the receipt and handed it to him.

"That will be all," she added, imperiously, and closed the door behind him.

After putting her shopping away, Angela fell into her sofa and opened the envelope. She was not surprised by

Undivulged Crimes

its contents: for reasons of public order, she and Boots would not be able to have their wedding in Golden Gate Park, or, indeed, in any other park in the city, or on the beach, pier, rocks, pavement or in the street.

Clearly, she and Boots would have to make alternative arrangements.

Angela went to her desk and turned on her laptop for the first time in several days. She did not open her email, but launched her browser and went to her once wholly ignored webpages.

"My wedding to Boots will not now take place in Golden Gate Park. An alternative venue is being arranged for a small, private ceremony," she typed, then reached for the gin.

Two days later, Angela dared to put her telephone back on the hook. She didn't know if it would connect or not, but she didn't really care. When she dared to look at her LookAtMe site again, there were several hundred messages of support and only a few that said, "Die Bitch" or "Cats are for Curry." Many messages were sympathetic, expressing disbelief that someone could be treated like this in the 21st century. (All right, they had said 20th century, but the thought was there.)

She had considered adding her latest thoughts about her wedding, but, in fact, she had had none. No solution was presenting itself, so she wrote, "Thank you for sharing your kind thoughts," and left it at that.

Angela's Wedding

Angela and Boots had a quiet supper and watched a DVD of *Amelie*. She loved its feel-good optimism, the hint of mystery, gentle humor and Parisian setting. When it finished, she double-checked the doors and went to bed.

The next morning, she awoke with her problem solved.

At least she thought she had solved it until there was a persistent knocking on her door shortly after eleven.

"This is the police officer watching your house," the voice shouted. "There's a man here with a lawful reason to speak with you. Open up!"

She complied.

A man in a cheap suit stood there with a briefcase.

"My name is Tyler Karshian and I represent the interests of Brandon and Cody Kristos," he said, pompously.

She doubted Tyler was his given name. His mother's maiden name in a pinch; or her first name; but, Brandon and Cody she knew about and had wondered when they'd crawl out of the woodwork.

"May I come in?"

"No," she replied, simply and without hostility.

She'd dealt with the Kristos' lawyers before. This was a new one.

"I am instructed to tell you that a preliminary injunction has been taken out preventing your proposed nuptials until the court has had the opportunity to rule on its validity. Failure to comply may result in being held in contempt of court," he said, handing her the document.

She looked at it.

"This injunction is against me," she said.

"That is correct."

"Where is the one against Boots?"

Karshian looked confused.

"I understand that I am prevented from marrying, but if there is no other injunction, Boots is not," she said with feigned confidence. "According to this, there is nothing to prevent Boots from marrying me."

This should cost the Kristos sibling a few hundred dollars more.

Karshian sighed.

"Miss Romano," he began wearily. "We both know what this is about. Athena Kristos left her fortune to her cat, and you were named as the cat's primary guardian and carer. Mrs. Kristos was grateful to you for looking after her for so long and wanted a way of giving you a stipend."

"And I remain grateful," Angela said. "I pray for her soul and light a candle for her every month."

"I am sure everyone is grateful," Karshian sighed. "However, everyone also knows that if you marry the cat, half the fortune becomes immediately yours, and when it dies, you will, without impediment, inherit the balance."

"Are there people who are so cynical?" she asked,

Angela's Wedding

sweetly. "That's very sad. I shall pray for them, too."

Karshian almost audibly counted to ten.

"You may pray for them all you want, but you will not succeed in your scheme."

"I'm not sure what you're suggesting, Mr. Karshian," Angela said, and looked towards the police officer who had returned to the pavement. "Officer! Could you please come here. I believe I am being threatened and would like a witness to what Mr. Tyler Karshian has just said to me. Would you repeat it, please. For the officer."

Karshian didn't make it to ten this time.

"Good-bye, Miss Romano."

She tossed the injunction with her junk mail, resolving to always write the word as injunktion.

In the kitchen, Angela had another cup of coffee and smiled to herself. The injunktion would not affect her plans at all.

In the afternoon, she cleaned Boots' travel carrier and unwrapped and cleaned the travel water bottle she had bought from Limpopo a few weeks earlier. She cut a section of spare carpet for the floor of the carrier and fitted it snugly.

"Boots!" she called, and the cat looked up sleepily.

Angela took one of Boots' favorite toys, laced with catnip, and bounced it into the carrier, which was followed without hesitation by Boots after only the fifth attempt. However, she seemed to like the feel of the new

Undivulged Crimes

carpet as well as the smell of the toy and settle down inside the carrier.

This was going well, Angela thought.

Two days later, Angela and Boots boarded a Shoshone Air Services (SAS-US) flight from San Francisco's Richard Nixon International Airport and flew to Las Vegas.

There were no problems, except they would only sell her two gin and tonics during the ninety-minute flight. She had only carry-on luggage and Boots so was able to make her way to the Trump International Hotel with minimal fuss.

That evening, she'd given herself a strict limit to the amount she'd let herself gamble. This was a happy and lucky time for her, and she managed to win just under five hundred dollars playing blackjack before a few more drinks and bed.

After all, it was a big day tomorrow.

Boots looked terrific: brushed and fresh, she was ready for her big day, and so was Angela. What made things even better was that no one had let the cat out of the bag, and she and Boots went unaccosted.

When the taxi pulled up to the Blue Moon Wedding Chapel with a dream in her heart, her denim skirt, tall boots with four-inch heels, fringed waistcoat, embroidered shirt, tooled leather belt with turquoise and silver accessories, Angela's childhood wedding-day dreams were realized.

Angela's Wedding

Sitting at the back of the chapel with other couples awaiting the services of the Officiating Colonel, Angela had the chance to reflect on how well things had gone. The venue was perfect; she looked perfect, and the injunction only covered California.

She saw two sweet weddings in the fifteen minutes she waited, and before her wedding was announced. She had paid the fee and signed the documents. She had given Boots to the clerk who pressed her paws on an ink pad and placed on the document. There would be no accusations of deception or coercion.

She walked up the aisle proudly, carrying Boots who was clearly agreeable, lulled by the tones of the King crooning "I Can't Help Falling in Love with You."

There were the basic questions. No one objected, and Boots meow-ed as if on cue.

The King sang a few bars (the maximum allowed without violating copyright, or delaying the awaiting couples) of "Love Me Tender" as the final bits of bureaucracy were carried out.

And they were married, and everyone clapped and smiled.

Having been lulled by the King's velvet tones, the blast of the final number startled Boots who leapt from Angela's arms and darted down the aisle, out the door and into the street to accompanying sounds of rubber violently sliding on asphalt; metal meeting metal; glass

Undivulged Crimes

encountering a variety of hard objects, and gasps from the congregation.

Perhaps "Hound Dog" wasn't the best choice for a recessional, but it had always been one of her favorites, and this was the happiest day of her life, wasn't it?

Undivulged Crimes

Undivulged Crimes

Undivulged Crimes

Undivulged Crimes

The first humid heat of the season rose from the earth and hovered along the coast on the day I arrived at Flanders. I felt most uncomfortable after the four-hour drive and my linen suit would do with a cleaning once I'd settle in. Not for at least a dozen years had I arrived at Flanders in such mugginess.

It was my forty-fifth consecutive summer at the hotel, and the sixtieth year since my first visit with my parents. There had been many changes over the years, so many, in fact, that I now felt things were just about the same as they were when I spent my first summer on the gulf coast of Louisiana.

The work of my lifetime has taken me around the world three times and I have lived for several years in five different countries; but for the summers – ah! – the summers were always spent at Flanders. Whether I would move from my mountain home in Northern California, or fly from a rented villa in Spain, June, July and August had to be spent at Flanders.

The summer weather was dreadful: hot, humid, and without a whisper of air for days. Then, there would be summer storms which one would expect to tear the trees out by the roots and level the long wood-frame building that was Flanders.

Flanders had been built at the turn of the century as a small, family-run summer resort hotel. It could have remained open all year, and done handsomely, too, but that wasn't Flanders. Flanders was for people who lived ordered, leisurely, lives; people who controlled their destinies, and would make themselves free for those months that the hotel was open – or at least for one month.

Much of the original furniture still filled the hotel, which had been extended in two directions from the original building. Now, it arches two wings towards the beach, and extends its vine-covered veranda *cum* promenade, three-hundred-fifty feet across the front, and an equal length across the side facing the beach.

At one time, there were palm trees between the beach and the hotel. A storm in the late forties swept them away along with most of the gardens. In time, the gardens were restored, but not the palms.

There were palms inside Flanders, however. I don't expect there was a time since its opening that there weren't palms in the lobby, around the dining room and on the staircases. Most of the gas fixtures were still in evidence, though wired for electricity. (At times, the current behaved much as it did sixty years ago, for it seemed that with the least breeze the lines would be down and Flanders would be plunged into darkness).

Undivulged Crimes

But it was not only Flanders itself that didn't change; the people who visited summer after summer were always the same. Most of them – nay, most of *us* – are fairly old now. Each year there are fewer and fewer of the old crowd. The news during the first weeks of summer is never good. It is the news of who is not coming this year, and who is no longer alive.

I examine the small library for a new book, but there isn't one. There hasn't been one for twenty years. The only changes are the ones which get lost, and the ones I leave behind when I go in August.

My room, the same one I had as a boy when on vacation with my parents, faces the gulf. It is on the fourth and top floor of the hotel where the heat is greatest. But, I can see for miles across the water, and for miles down the beach. It looks the same now as it did in 1917, except for the palms.

Flanders is isolated on a patch of sand separated from the mainland by a marshy area which joins the gulf at its edges. There is one road, one low bridge and one town on the islet. Nearly a thousand acres at the far end of this over-grown sandbar belong to Flanders.

Although little grows naturally immediately around the hotel, there is dense growth on both sides of the drive, which makes the shock of seeing a long, lone building amid sand, sea and sky the greater. Carved out of the

Undivulged Crimes

jungle are tennis courts, croquet lawns and long, quiet paths to stroll when the mosquitoes aren't too thick.

Parties were given there, too. Parties, with colored lights, and dance bands all the way from Baton Rouge and New Orleans. Boys from the best schools in the south, and belles.

I remember the summer shortly before the war began. I watched from a tree, being too young to attend myself. I still experience a pang of horrified innocence at what took place beneath my tree branch during the course of the evening. It was not easy to reconcile the façade with the reality at the age of twelve. Not in those days, at least. It would only be a few years before I would be beneath that tree, I thought with bravado. I, of course, would take great care to examine the branches overhead.

It was not to be. The war intervened. My parents did not return to Flanders for another six years and society had changed.

Though, in a backward, looking-glass sort of way, things were yet the same. Flanders was here. Marion Cassidy was still spending her summers here. In fact, we still took cocktails together from time to time. Norma Wilson is still here – three husbands later; and Mirabell Murray Hopkins, who as a girl was escorted by me to a grand summer dance on the tennis court.

Undivulged Crimes

Norma told me, when I saw her on the veranda, that Harry Lee Prescott wouldn't be coming until late July because Julia had died in May.

Horace McNab was there again with his mother. Horace was sixty-nine and Mama was ninety-three. Mama, as always, was in far better health than Horace. Poor Horace lived all his life in her shadow. The family wealth enabled them to maintain a pre-World War I style of living to the present day, but the comfort kept Horace at Magnolia, pottering about its lawns and gardens, never to see the real world, or dull an ounce of his imagination – which was never thought to be much anyway.

The heat was unbroken. Dinner was served on the veranda. The flowers on the table drooped by dessert, and mosquitoes buzzed under the broad brims of straw hats. Rocking gently on the front porch in the coming coolness after dinner, Marion Cassidy sat next to me. Marion had never married. I had known her since the 1917 summer and gone swimming with her several times, although I was twelve and she was nearly sixteen. It was Marion who gave me the first hint of what it must have been like beneath secluded trees.

I was twenty when I saw Marion again. She was a spinster. She had become engaged to a boy from her home town who had been killed in the war. She withdrew from everything, and vowed never to marry. It sounds a

Undivulged Crimes

cliché, still, it's what people did in those days, and it was no cliché to Marion.

My father died in 1925. My mother bravely decided to summer at Flanders the following year. She was unable to endure what must have been grand memories, and I received a telegram to retrieve her. She died the following spring.

I began to travel. There was money, and there were a few prosperous places in the world. I decided to spend the dark days from 1929 to 1936 abroad. I toured India and China, investing a little money, and getting much more back. In August 1932, I returned to Flanders, fell in love, and have returned every summer since.

Most people were involved in two social sets in the affluent – decadent, if you must – South: a winter set, around one's area; and a summer set, people one saw only at resort hotels. In rare instances, there were people whom you saw the whole year round, which became tedious.

My love was pure summer sets. Margaret May Cross. Her mother wasn't altogether certain about us, but we paid little attention. After three months under as many trees as we could find, we wrote voluminously to each other for nine months, until Flanders opened again.

Margaret May had a sister who was not quite right. Rumors were that she was locked in the attic rooms of

Undivulged Crimes

their Georgia home, all but abandoned during the summer months.

Never did Margaret May mention her; never did I ask; I suspect it was true, for when her mother died, Margaret May failed to appear at Flanders for two years.

I nearly despaired. It was dreadful to face the summer without her. I thought of going to Crossways, in Georgia, but summer wouldn't be summer if it weren't spent at Flanders. I felt I must wait to see what appeared on the veranda overlooking the gulf.

The parties continued. The jazz blared on, and people and fashions became more daring.

One night, in the early hours, after a roaring party, a shot echoed through the hotel.

The cause of Gerald Wilbanks' suicide was never clearly established. Dr. Drew had been in the suite across the hall, and found the body. Rose was still sleeping off the party in the bedroom.

Drink, drugs, too much pressure from a bookmaker or bootlegger, or the fear of the discovery of some other indiscretion – these were all speculated on at length, but resolved neither by the coroner nor the residents of Flanders. His widow, still lives handsomely on the insurance, and stays in the same room every year at Flanders.

Colonel Jackson stopped to chat to me after breakfast on my second morning. He had become a colonel in 1933, and conveniently retired from the army in 1939. I doubt

Undivulged Crimes

he did anything more than play with lead soldiers since then. He had been in a famous Great War battle, and decorated.

The Flanders society was curious. Some of us had known each other for more than fifty years, yet, there were few intimate relationships. There had been, of course, in the days when we were young and beautiful, but now – now, we just simply knew each other; what we did; how much we drank; how many times we'd been married.

Flanders was old ghosts, old lovers, old secrets. Margaret May was my own personal ghost. Even now when I first glimpse Flanders against the hot white sky and pale sand, the feeling that she is there comes back as strong as ever.

Margaret May still never mentions her sister. When people spoke about Laura, it was never in a cruel or malicious way, but rather of the "poor girls," which sympathized with victim, daughter and mother.

Despite the lack of evidence for the mad sister, there was certainly no doubt that Margaret May's mother would forbid anything more than a summer acquaintance between us. After several frustrating years, we grew apart.

༄

One of the first people I talked to this year was Marion Cassidy. We rocked in our chairs watching the fading

Undivulged Crimes

sky. Marion told me much of the year's news, as she had heard it. The dining room head is queer, but so is the new cook; and he's even such a good cook that they'd get along and not both quit.

"Norma's back again, too. All her husbands – and do you think she's happy?" she continued. "Well, I suppose we both ended up in the same place anyway."

We chatted about books, and a little winter news, but not much. She mentioned that Horace and his mother were back, along with a number of others. There were a few more new people, but she didn't suppose they'd stay for more than a few days.

"How could they enjoy themselves here? This place is ours. This place is us."

Just before midnight, a thunderstorm erupted and plunged the hotel into darkness.

"Nothing really changes, does it?" said a voice coming towards me in the dark.

"Always the same," I said. Then, as we came closer, "Yes. Who's that? Ah! How good to see you – ah, well, *hear* you, at least. Do come talk to me in the morning. I'm usually on the east terrace until eleven. Good night. Safe trip."

I lay in my bed and listened to the thunder roll and watched the old beach house light up brighter than life. Later, when I awoke, the sound of thunder had given way

Undivulged Crimes

to the sound of heavy rain. At dawn, there was only the sound of the sea.

Horace, whom I had bumped into in the night, looked much the same as ever as he sat on the terrace in the morning sun. Already brown roasted, he wore a panama hat and a linen jacket. He was reading a newspaper.

Feelings for Horace had changed over the decades. In youth, we thought he was babyish, pampered and not altogether intelligent. Later on, we thought he was just weak and unable to break the psychological bonds which his mother used to tie him to her, and to Magnolia.

I had come to find Horace to be intelligent, kind and hopelessly innocent. He had been deprived of experience and for that was he really to be blamed?

Magnolia was the womb to him, and he had no wish, and no need, to leave it.

Little was known about the romance between Horace and Laura. Indeed, I was never certain if such a romance ever occurred, since I was never certain of Laura's existence. The rumor was that Laura had not been considered odd before it. But, that was supposedly in 1924, and Horace would have been only sixteen then.

"Fewer and fewer every year," Horace was saying. "I made a count last night during the storm, when Mama couldn't sleep. I first came here in 1920. You had been coming for some time then."

"Since 1917."

Undivulged Crimes

"Marion Cassidy first came in 1917, too," Horace said. "She told me last year. She knew you then."

I nodded, wondering how much people had told Horace over the years. We tell things to people whom we do not expect to remember or understand.

"Rose Wilbanks first came in 1921, and Norma Wilson, whatever-her-name-is now, came late that summer."

"When did the Crosses first come?"

I watched Horace, but he made no reaction.

"Nineteen-twenty-two," he said reflectively. "Of course, Mrs Cross died in 1930, and Margaret May has been coming since."

"Colonel Jackson first came in 1939, didn't he?"

"Yes. He had been here for a few days just after the big war, but didn't return until he retired."

"Did you know Franklin, Marion's fiancé?"

"No. He was dead before I ever came here," he said.

"You didn't know him anywhere else?"

"Oh, no. I don't know anyone except here." He paused. "I did hear all about it, though. Laura told me. She was a friend of Marion, and mine."

He gave a brief smile.

It struck me that he and I could have been brothers-in-law – or whatever that relationship would have been– had we married the Misses Cross we wanted to. Had Mrs Cross thwarted him as she had me?

Undivulged Crimes

"There are others," Horace went on. "Aurelia Fayr, Herbert Quinn, Dr. Drew and Miss Brady, but you really aren't friendly with them, are you?"

"We're not old friends," I admitted.

"Mother never liked Aurelia Fayr, and Herbert Quinn's daughter had been foul to me when I was fifteen. Things like that have their consequences.

"Nice people, really. Dr. Drew was an old friend of Rose and Gerald Wilbanks. Remember Gerald? Tragedy."

Conversations were nearly the same year after year. it made one young again to close one's eyes, listen to familiar voices tell familiar stories. Great pleasure.

In the dining room, I saw Margaret May with Marion Cassidy. I greeted them and we had coffee together after lunch. They were in good form. Margaret May had also arrived the day before, and was fresh with news of family and friends.

"My nephew," Margaret May was saying, "has just left Duke with his degree and is going into the Air Force. He'll be an officer. Of course, he's not really a nephew, but my mother's sister's grandchild, but he's been a nephew to me. He wants to get into the squadron that used to be the old 'Stars and Bars' squadron of the Air Service. He's got everyone writing letters to Washington to pull it off."

"I'll bet he's very proud," I said.

"I'm very proud of him," Margaret May said.

Undivulged Crimes

She took out a picture of her almost nephew and showed it to us.

Marion took her customary handful of pills with her last swallow of coffee and we left the dining room.

Later that day, I passed Marion in the garden. She gripped my arm, looked straight into my eyes and said proudly:

"Franklin was in the 'Stars and Bars' squadron, too," she said.

Nothing further was said and she continued her walk across the lawn.

I continued on to the beach. I still like to swim, though I'm no longer fit. The beach was deserted. Such a waste, for it's a beautiful, long, clean beach. There were parties on the beach, as well as on the tennis courts, and there was fun in the sand, as well as under the trees.

The gray timbers of the pavilion still rose from the top of a sand dune and a corner of carving, an oriental animal face, now silver-gray, peered out to sea in silence.

Margaret May had had a birthday party there in the twenties. There were state senators and parish officials. There was also a great amount of liquor, too. It was the sort of party that had made prohibition come true.

I climbed the dune; the original steps were lost under the sand. There was more of the pavilion showing than there had been in years. The sands had shifted and the floor was nearly clear. It had been highly polished

Undivulged Crimes

parquet, but now only weather- beaten broad boards remained. Only a few tiles remained on the roof and the sky looked in on all sides.

In one corner, some posts rose from the floor. They had supported a long smooth bar, backed by a mirrored and marbled dresser with shining brass.

I struggled to hear strains of old music. None. Children calling to each other in the distance caused an unexpected jolt, however. A music that does not change. Was it on that night, the night of Margaret May's birthday, that Laura ran across the dunes into the darkness, dropping clothing? That was the story, at least. Could that have been the Horace McNab affair?

Was Laura "all right" then? Was that the summer of 1924? I would have been nineteen; the party would have been Margaret May's nineteenth birthday party; Laura would have been fifteen. It could have been that party.

But, it could have been earlier, or later. . . .

I wonder what Horace and Laura did? I wouldn't have thought ordinary sex would have knocked a southern girl into life-long dementia.

Lama-like, I sat on the floor of the ruined pavilion, gazing out to sea, following the same steady sightlines as the carved beast above me.

Do you remember, old tiger? Do you?

It was bridge night at the hotel. I only play during the summer, and so am never very successful, but there are a few people who don't mind playing with me. That night I found Colonel Jackson at my table. He was a fine player, and I rose to his standard once or twice, but played consistently better than usual.

The colonel and I played against Dr. Drew and Rose Wilbanks.

"I don't know how I got on to the men's table," she said. "I certainly don't play like a man."

She was an independent little woman. She, too, played very well. It was her game. Her pastime. Her life.

"Rose, you know why you're playing here," the doctor said. "They won't have you anywhere else."

"Don't be rude, Joseph," she said with a slight pout. "What will the colonel think."

"Two no trump."

"Three clubs."

"Pass."

"Five clubs."

"Dummy again," said Dr. Drew.

The hand was played and won by Rose. So was the rubber. The second rubber was won by the colonel and Rose. The third, by Rose and me.

I had a late drink with the colonel on the northern porch.

"Shrewd woman," Colonel Jackson said. "I doubt much would get past her."

Undivulged Crimes

"I shouldn't think so," I replied. "I guess she's had to learn to be self-sufficient."

"Why's that?"

"Being a widow so young."

"Oh. Right. I see what you mean. Of course, that was before my time. I did know her husband, though."

"Had you been here earlier?"

"No. Gerald Wilbanks had been in the Air Service with me in the Great War."

"Small world."

"Another funny thing was that I knew the brother of a girl who used to come here, too. Met her here one summer after the war. Her brother stayed in the Air Service, same as me, but I never saw him again - nor her."

He knocked back his drink and we retired.

Two mornings later, we were greeted by a sight which, though not uncommon, was one which struck fear into our pre-war hearts. A hearse was parked at the foot of the front steps, the rear with its maw gaping, awaiting its victim.

Although a dozen or more of us stood at the railing looking down, no one dared ask for whom it had been summoned. If people were to die, why couldn't they do it in their own homes, and not here, where they shattered our poor illusion of youth. Why couldn't they die in the winter when most old people do? It was upsetting. Cruel. Inconsiderate.

Undivulged Crimes

"Marion Cassidy," someone said.

"Heart attack."

I noticed Horace standing next to me.

"'*Then be not coy, but use your time, For, having lost but once your prime, You may forever tarry.*' Excuse me," said Horace and quickly departed.

The irony of Horace's quiet perception stayed in my mind for the next few days. There was now one less in our crowd. We all felt it, but there was nothing to be done. The body was shipped back to Vidalia. None of us knew if she had any relatives. There was no funeral, no letters, flowers or wreaths. She just left us quietly.

When I eventually saw Dr. Drew, the entire episode had already worked itself into Flanders history. They talked about Marion as though she had been dead for years, not just a few days.

"It was her heart," the doctor said. "She'd been on her pills for years, but it takes more than a little digitalis or strychnine to keep a heart going."

"Was anyone there?"

"She had spent the early part of the evening with Rose, but had gone to her room fairly early. Rose stopped in later, found her and called me. She had been dead for at least an hour by then."

"Poor Rose."

Undivulged Crimes

"It was a dreadful shock to her. I've put her on a very mild sedative until the shock passes. They had been close friends for years."

Margaret May was upset by Marion's death, too. She had been an even closer friend than Rose. I suppose they shared the secrets of spinsterhood. Margaret May's life and Marion's – and even Horace's – were much the same. They were lived in the shadow of the existence of a more powerful being. Margaret May and Horace had their mothers whom they could not escape. Marion had her Franklin, whose spirit never left her.

I, of course, am in the control of Flanders and all that has gone before in the summers since my youth. What a sad collection of broken pieces is life. Are there no complete patterns?

Horace sat on the east terrace a week after Marion's death. I hadn't spoken to him since that morning on the porch.

"Mama says she's been waiting for Marion to die for years, I said, 'Mama, what a dreadful thing to say!' But she told me that she always thought there was something funny between Marion and Rose Wilbanks."

"Funny?"

"I never noticed. But Mama's a clever woman. Mind like a trap. She immediately saw the irony of it all."

"Irony?"

Undivulged Crimes

"Maybe you don't remember: Marion's body was found by Rose. Years ago, Rose's husband's body was found by Marion."

"I thought old Drew found it."

"No. Marion's room was next door. She heard the shot, entered the room, saw Gerald – without the few brains he ever had – and sent for Drew. Just about forty years ago. To the day, Mama says. Curious, the pattern things have."

On the veranda, I mulled over the curious pattern. It was a subtle, southern pattern. Delicate, elusive, fleeting. I was beginning to perceive some logic to it all – or at least fancied I perceived something, when Colonel Jackson came along with his newspaper.

"Aircraft lost over Texas because a goose flew through the windshield. What nonsense. When I flew, we rarely had a windshield. Good open air bi-planes. Great stuff. . . ."

He droned on for several minutes about the old days of aviation, then launched an attack on modern planes.

". . . reduced pilots to button-pushers. No real need for them anymore. Only around to take the blame if someone gets killed. A dying breed – say, did you hear, Margaret May's nephew is joining my old squadron?"

"That's right. You were in the 'Stars and Bars'?"

"I told you I knew Gerald."

"Yes, of course."

Undivulged Crimes

"Poor boy. Had too much rank for his own good. Had to give orders which no man his age should have had to. Sent two thirds of a squadron to their deaths. Controversial mission. War is hell. I was on the ground that day. Foul war. The Frenchies and the British don't think we suffered."

"Then you knew Franklin, Marion's fiancé, too?"

"Goodness, yes. Fine fellow. He was killed in that sortie I just mentioned."

Patterns. Patterns, I thought:

In a month he would have been my husband.
In a month, here, underneath this lime,
We would have broken the pattern;
He for me, and I for him;
He a colonel, I as lady,
On this shady seat.
He had a whim
That sunlight carried blessing.
And I answered, 'It shall be as you have said.'
Now he is dead. . . ."

Franklin is dead. Gerald is dead. Marion is dead.

And I know why.

Perhaps Rose knows that I know. If not, what will she do if she does?

I sit beneath the pavilion roof. Great tiger, have you seen it all?

I have solved an ancient puzzle by accident.

Undivulged Crimes

The carved, worn, wooden head stares out to sea.

There were once four. Did one of them see Marion Cassidy kill Gerald Wilbanks in 1924? Did it know it was because Wilbanks had commanded the action that killed Franklin?

Did Rose figure this out last week during the conversation about Margaret May's ersatz nephew? Rose so easily could have given Marion an overdose of her medicine.

And what of poor Horace and Laura? Tell me, beast, was that, too, part of the pattern?

Too improbable; too bizarre. The wooden beast retains the undivulged crimes it has witnessed. Retains them, unwhipped, and so do I.

I grow afraid of Flanders. I know the solution to a five decade-old murder, and a fresh one, too.

The evil taints all around me. What else has happened here? Horace and Laura? Margaret May and me?

Flanders, always bitter-sweet. Now, more bitter. Already, in late June, I must think about next year. Can I come back again? Or is this world too hopelessly drawn to the present?

I am not an old lama. Merely an old fool, sitting on the decayed floor of a tumbled pavilion at an antiquated resort.

But I am not afraid, for I look up at the great Chinese tiger and see that the beast is blind.

Undivulged Crimes

The End

By the same author:

Entrusted in Confidence
The three entertainments following the events of *The Countess Comes Home. The Countess' Secret, The Brentano Affair* and *Bill Bradley Rides Again* continue to explore personal, moral and ethical dilemmas against a background of the secret service.

On the Edge of Dreams and Nightmares
An award-winning tale of child-abuse, incest, madness and murder: Ligeia Gordon's solution to her deep psychological troubles is to infiltrate the life of the distinguished painter, Sir Nigel Thomas, an older man who has his own ghosts to contend with.

Portland Place: A novel from Jane Austen's Lost Years
Jane Austen meets the Americans. In the "era of good feeling," Nora Woodruff finds herself in London for the first time, and encountering citizens of the new nation. Manners and attitudes conflict against a background of rising political tension.

Undivulged Crimes

The Countess Comes Home

At the end of the Vietnam War, Lieutenant (j.g.) Bill Bradley is ordered to deliver documents from Yankee Station to Saigon, to an enigmatic young woman he knows only as "the countess." Decades later, the shadow of that mission falls on his retirement when a message is received saying that the countess wants to come home.

Nantucket Summer

From the haunted residents of the darkened rooms of the unpainted Hardwicke mansion, Midwestern waitresses, and the retreats of the establishment, to the creeping, *nouveau riche* infiltrators with their oversized, post-modern houses and competitive spirits, *Nantucket Summer* is a memoir of those who summered on the wood-framed New England coast in the 1960s.

Wachusett

In the summer of 1876, the nation prepares to mark its centennial. Marion Easton travels from her Boston home to a resort hotel on Mount Wachusett in central Massachusetts where she joins her future in-laws and their family. However, as July 4 approaches, there is little to celebrate.

Undivulged Crimes

The Camels of the Qur'an

The death of a BBC journalist, a missing girl, and an unpublished novel, lead the reluctant David Powell into a labyrinth of Middle Eastern customs, politics and intrigue. Determined to discover if his friend's death was an accident, or murder, Powell finds his familiar reference points gone, and nothing quite what it seems.

Watch for:

The Rock Pool

The power of a special place can become a lasting influence, and when combined with the experience of love, it shape the future. Nick Lucas' love for the unobtainable Sarah Hallam becomes the unwelcome centre of his life.

The Lost Lady

Art, music and intrigue provide the backdrop to the tangle of lost loyalties and loves in *années folles* Paris. Jazz and surrealism drink coffee and wine with politics, ambition, fear and lost identities. Emigrés and refugees look for meaning, but settle for survival and another drink.

Undivulged Crimes

Undivulged Crimes

Undivulged Crimes

Printed in Poland
by Amazon Fulfillment
Poland Sp. z o.o., Wrocław